PEERING THROUGH THE WINDOW, OZ COULD SEE NO SIGN OF XANDER OR JUSTINE.

"What are you doing?" a sharp female voice demanded.

Oz turned slowly to face the artist. "Looking for Xander, actually. No one answered the door."

Justine tucked several packages under one arm and reached into a pocket with her free hand. "Xander went home over an hour ago."

"Thanks. I'll check there." Oz accidentally jostled Justine's arm as he passed and two of the items fell to the ground. He and the artist both stooped to pick them up, but he touched a deck of cards.

A sizzling tingle rushed from his hand into the deck. A wave of dizziness overwhelmed him, and he fell back against the wall. He blinked to clear his head, but everything was fuzzy.

Justine opened the door and stood back. "Come in, Oz."

Oz swayed slightly. His entire awareness was suddenly focused on the calm, compelling sound of Justine's voice.

He wanted to refuse.

He walked into the room against his will.

MEDIA TIE-INS

Buffy the Vampire Slayer™

Available from ARCHWAY Paperbacks and POCKET PULSE

Buffy the Vampire Slayer adult books

Available from POCKET BOOKS

BUFFY
THE VAMPIRE
SLAYER™

DOOMSDAY DECK

Diana G. Gallagher

An original novel based on the hit TV series created by Joss Whedon

POCKET PULSE
New York   London   Toronto   Sydney   Singapore

HISTORIAN'S NOTE:

This story takes place during
the third season.

This book is a work of fiction. Names, characters, places and
incidents are products of the author's imagination or are used
fictitiously. Any resemblance to actual events or locales or persons,
living or dead, is entirely coincidental.

An *Original* Publication of POCKET BOOKS

 POCKET PULSE, published by
Pocket Books, a division of Simon & Schuster, Inc.
1230 Avenue of the Americas, New York, NY 10020

™ and copyright © 2000 by Twentieth Century Fox Film
Corporation. All rights reserved.

ISBN: 0-7434-0041-0

First Pocket Pulse printing December 2000

10 9 8 7 6 5 4 3 2 1

POCKET PULSE and colophon are registered
trademarks of Simon & Schuster, Inc.

Printed in the U.S.A.

Fondly for Helen Baumander,
my good friend in the North Country

Acknowledgments

The author gratefully acknowledges the following people for their assistance: my agent, Ricia Mainhardt, and her partner, A.J. Janschewitz, for always being there when I need them; my mother, Beryl M. Turner, and Betsey Wilcox for proofreading and keeping me on track; my husband, Martin R. Burke, for his continued support; my editor, Lisa Clancy, for her guidance, patience, and confidence; and Lisa's assistant, Micol Ostow, for answering questions promptly and efficiently.

Special thanks to Tabitha Baumander for providing information on Tarot at the beginning of this project and to Janice Scott-Reeder for the character Tarot readings incorporated into the manuscript. The author is solely responsible for any mistakes or misinterpretations.

I am especially grateful to Joss Whedon and the cast and crew of *Buffy the Vampire Slayer* for their creative efforts and inspiration.

DOOMSDAY DECK

CHAPTER 1

Buffy checked her bad mood along with her jacket when she entered The Vineyard, a small Italian restaurant located just around the corner from her mother's art gallery.

"Buffy!" Papa Joe Felucci, the elderly owner, beamed when he saw her. "Where have you been? We haven't seen you in weeks!"

"I was getting fat on Felucci fettucini." Buffy smiled, warmed by the old man's friendly smile. She and her mom had been regular customers since they had moved to Sunnydale.

"Impossible!" Joe feigned a look of shocked dismay. "My fettucini is almost calorie free!"

"Good! Because my stomach has been grumbling for it all day." Buffy laughed and followed Joe into the dining room. When her mom had invited her to dinner, she had eagerly accepted, hoping the diversion would take her mind off exams.

"Buffy!" Joyce Summers waved from a corner table by a large bay window. Festive lanterns illuminated the grape arbors in the small courtyard outside. Her mother's smile lit up the room.

"Sorry I'm late." Buffy gave Joyce a peck on the cheek and sat down. "Can we order right away? I'm famished."

"Didn't you eat lunch?" Joyce asked with a frown, then shook her hand to erase the inquiry. "Never mind. I promised myself I wouldn't indulge in any maternal meddling tonight."

"No third degree?" Buffy teased. "What will we talk about?"

"I'll think of something." Joyce smiled and scanned the menu. "After I decide on one of Joe's specialties."

Buffy knew the menu by heart and handed it to the waiter unopened. "Antipasto, Felucci fettucini, and iced tea."

"Make it two." Joyce sighed when the waiter left. She picked up a breadstick and broke it, then placed it on her bread plate and absently sipped her coffee.

Buffy thought she seemed a little tense. "So how was your day, Mom? Everything okay at the gallery?"

"Business is booming." Joyce nodded, smiled, and hesitated again.

"So why do I get the impression there's a problem?" Buffy asked.

"No problem," Joyce quickly countered. "Not yet, anyway."

"Anything I can do to help?" Buffy felt awkward pumping her mother for information, but something was obviously troubling her. "With whatever it is . . . that you don't want to tell me."

"What?" Joyce started. "Oh, no. I *want* to talk to you about it. That's why I asked you to dinner . . . and because we haven't been out together lately."

Buffy smiled to put her mother at ease. "So what do you need?"

Joyce put down the breadstick and looked Buffy in the eye. "The Slayer."

"Slayer? As in stake-a-vampire Slayer?" Buffy lowered her voice and frowned. "What vampire?"

"No one in particular," Joyce said. "The Sunnydale Sidewalk Art Festival is this weekend and, well, unlike most of the people in this town, *I* know we have a serious security problem."

"I forgot about the festival!" Buffy gave herself a mental slap to the forehead for spacing yet another of her mother's projects.

Since the previous festival coordinator was now a permanent resident of the Shady Hill Cemetery, Joyce had been asked to coordinate and run the weekend event. The City Council insisted on holding the Sidewalk Art Festival every year as though it might somehow prove Sunnydale was just an ordinary small town. Most of Sunnydale's population existed in a state of blind denial regarding the Hell-mouth horrors that stalked the streets.

Her mother didn't suffer from any such delusions.

Hard to ignore the demon underground when your daughter is the first and only line of defense, Buffy thought.

Joyce leaned forward to whisper. "I mean, what if some demon thing picks this weekend to launch a reign of terror?"

"Well, as far as I know, Giles isn't worried about anything big happening," Buffy offered, to ease her mother's mind.

Buffy, however, was mentally focused on Sunny-dale being overrun with unsuspecting artists and buyers. *Easy prey for the vampire gourmet,* she thought. "Serious security problem" hardly defined the potential for disaster. These days the sun set before seven. Lingering spectators and artists closing up their displays would be at great risk from vampires as darkness fell on downtown Sunnydale.

"Well, that's a relief, but—" Joyce glanced from side to side. "—what about vampires?"

"The normal menace?" Buffy shrugged. "If I concentrate my patrols around the show site and the nearby motels, I can probably keep the vamps under control."

Joyce sighed and nodded as she sat back. "I hate to ask you to give up your weekend, Buffy, but I really need your help. Nobody else can handle this except you and your friends."

Her mother's request was kind of ironic, Buffy realized. Six months ago Joyce had had a hard time accepting that her daughter was destined to defend the world against demonic evil until the day she died. Now Joyce needed her Slayer skills to safeguard the artists she had invited into the demons' lair.

"I don't have any plans," Buffy said. Actually, she was glad to have something to distract her from the tension that existed between her and Angel now. They didn't talk about it much, but the unsolvable problem was always there beneath the surface. They couldn't stand to be apart and yet, they were never really together.

"In fact," Buffy added, "I can't think of anything I'd rather do than help you out by dusting a few unsavory elements."

"Metaphorically speaking." Joyce smiled tightly as the waiter placed their appetizers in front of them.

"I'm pretty sure we can count on everyone to help out," Buffy said after the waiter left. "Giles, too, probably."

"I can't tell you what a relief that is." Joyce hesitated again. "Speaking of Willow and Xander, there is one other thing . . ."

"Name it." Buffy stabbed a piece of cheese and popped it into her mouth.

"I could use some brains and muscle with the actual art show," Joyce said. "I was hoping Willow might handle artist registration on the gallery computer. And maybe Oz and Xander could help mark off the display areas and help the artists set up?"

"I'll ask," Buffy said. "I'm meeting everyone at the Bronze later."

The Bronze was busy for a weeknight, but not packed to the rafters. Xander spotted Buffy and waved her over to the table he and Willow had grabbed near the stage. Willow's attention was glued to Oz as Dingoes Ate My Baby slammed into their break theme.

"Hey, Buffy!" Xander patted the chair beside him. "Welcome to the demon fighters anonymous social hour."

"Charter members only," Willow said. "Except for Oz."

"Did I miss something?" Buffy raised an eyebrow as she set down her coffee and slipped into the seat.

"Not unless you've got a thing for high stakes pool." Xander nodded toward the pool table. The Sunnydale High School basketball team had been challenged by a group of frat brats from the UC Sunnydale campus. "Loser buys—coffee all around."

A collective groan rose from the high school team when the fraternity challenger sank two balls with one stroke. The college boy slapped a high-five with a friend.

Buffy graced the competitive gathering with a casual look of disdain. "Like winning is a matter of life and death. I don't get it."

"It's a guy thing," Xander explained.

"Dingoes played two new songs in this set." Willow grinned. "And Devon only forgot the words twice."

"Four times." Oz pulled a chair over and kissed Willow on the cheek. "Five maybe."

"Not that anyone cares." Xander shrugged. "For someone who's several watts short of brilliant, Devon does a passable job of faking it."

"Then all's quiet in the demon department?" Buffy asked.

"It's so quiet I almost wish Spike would come back," Xander muttered. He looked up to find everyone staring. "To liven things up, which Spike does rather well for an undead guy."

"A little desperate for entertainment, aren't you?" Buffy blew on the steaming coffee and sipped.

Xander shrugged. Now that Cordelia Chase was romantic history, his status as an eligible senior male had resumed. Unfortunately, the only eligible female who seemed to care was Anya, an ex-demon with a passion for making men suffer.

"Then you don't have a hot date this weekend?" Buffy asked.

"Let me put it this way." Xander leaned forward. As of this second, he was still resisting Anya's not so subtle effort to attract him. "If the video store hasn't stocked up on new releases, it's going to be a very long, very boring weekend."

"We could always do popcorn and the monster movie marathon," Willow suggested. "Forty-eight hours of black and white classics starting at midnight Friday."

"Isn't the band booked?" Buffy glanced at Oz.

"Devon's going to LA to see an agent," Oz said. "No gig."

"No full moon and no snarly, hairy guy, either." Willow pressed closer to Oz.

"So you can neck without worrying about having your throat ripped out." Xander nodded. "We could hang out in my house. It's not Trump Plaza, but on the plus, it's totally parent free."

"And vampire safe," Oz said.

"Sounds like fun, but I was thinking more along the lines of sharpening some stakes and keeping the Sunnydale Sidewalk Art Festival vampire free." Buffy's gaze darted from one face to the other and settled on Xander.

Xander didn't hesitate. He'd seen every movie on the monster marathon schedule a dozen times. "Prime the crossbow and break out the holy water, I'm ready to ride."

"Great!" Buffy grinned. "And don't forget your hammer."

"What?" Xander frowned, confused. "We're going to pound the undead scum before we dust them?"

CHAPTER 2

The Gallery, which was serving as headquarters for the sidewalk art show, was bustling with activity. Buffy and Xander stood off to the side, out of the way as the other volunteer crews got their instructions and supplies from Joyce. Inside the office, Oz and Willow were disconnecting the computer. After a brief conference, they had decided to put the registration table in the main room off the entrance because it was more spacious and accessible than the office.

Xander paced, swinging a hammer. "This manual labor thing is like a disguise, right?"

"Right," Buffy said. "Between marking off the display sites today and helping the artists set up tomorrow, everyone will just assume we're part of the regular show staff. Which we are, in a way."

"Right. Undercover security." Xander shoved the hammer handle into his leather tool belt and folded his arms. "I like it."

Buffy smiled. What Xander lacked in skill he made up for with enthusiasm. *Which has almost gotten him killed a few too many times.*

"I'm going to go out and scout around a little." Xander checked the stakes stuffed into his back pockets. "Make sure there's no daylight demons lurking about in the alleys."

"Good idea. I'll be out as soon as Oz is ready." Buffy leaned against the wall as Xander sauntered outside.

Oz hustled out of the office carrying the computer monitor. Willow followed with other pieces and parts.

"I don't know what I'd do without you, Willow." Joyce stopped Willow and slipped a trailing cord onto the keyboard the girl carried. "All the other volunteers claimed computer ignorance, but I think they just wanted an excuse to get out of registration and operations. Sitting in the gallery all weekend won't be very exciting, I'm afraid."

Buffy stood up and stretched. The artist registration would be completed by Friday, but her mom needed someone in the gallery to coordinate the staff, direct any problems that arose to the pertinent person in charge, and dispense general information. Willow had graciously agreed to take on the responsibility.

"I'll bring a book or work on my physics paper,"

Willow said. "So I have something to do if things get boring, which I hope they do because, well, exciting in Sunnydale is usually fatal."

"Almost done, Buffy," Oz said as he dashed back into the office.

Joyce nodded in response to Willow's observation. "I know. It's just that I was so flattered when the City Council asked me to run this show, I didn't think about the dangers."

"Yeah, it's not like you can warn everyone." Willow pushed the monitor to the center of the table, then looked at an imaginary artist. "Oh, and by the way, Sunnydale has a little vampire problem. So it might be a good idea to, uh—carry a wooden stake and a cross with you . . . after dark only, of course."

Joyce smiled in spite of her concerns.

"Don't worry, Mom." Buffy picked up a floppy disk that had fallen and set it on the table. It was too bad her mother hadn't scheduled the show for Halloween weekend when demons usually went to ground. If this Sunnydale Sidewalk Art Festival went off without a massacre, she'd suggest it for next year. "We're on it."

Oz set the PC tower on the floor under the table and turned to Buffy. "Computer's moved. Now what?"

"We've got a whole city block to mark off." Buffy pulled a diagram of the city streets out of her pocket and pointed to a box by the door. "Grab that, will you?"

"Got it." Hefting the box, Oz followed Buffy outside.

Buffy saw Xander sitting on the bench in front of Walter's Deli before he saw them. Chin propped on his hands, his gaze focused on the street, he looked lost in thought. *Troubled?* Buffy wondered, glancing up and down the street. *Or waiting in ambush for a demon to pop out of thin air?*

"Doughnuts?" Oz called out.

Xander held up a bag. "Would the snacks guy let you down?"

"It's three o'clock in the afternoon!" Buffy exclaimed lightly. "You guys are going to rot away from the inside out."

"Then we'll blend right in with the walking corpses." Xander offered Buffy the bag.

Munching a Bavarian cream, Buffy led the way down the main street that constituted downtown Sunnydale. Using the diagrams Joyce had provided, the other groups of volunteers had begun attaching site markers to storefronts, telephone poles, and lampposts. Each preregistered artist already had been assigned a twelve-foot-long section of prime sidewalk display space. Last minute entrants would have to settle for lower profile areas on the designated side streets.

When they reached the corner of Main and Vista, Oz and Xander measured off the first spot and marked the boundaries with masking tape. Buffy rummaged through the box looking for the numbered space sign that corresponded to her site diagram.

"When does this show start?" Xander asked.

"Noon Friday. Runs through six P.M. Sunday." Buffy handed Xander the sign.

Xander nailed the sign to a tree at the edge of the display area, then spun his hammer and deftly slipped it back into his tool belt. His gaze swept the line of cars waiting for the light to change. "Won't traffic be a problem?"

"They're blocking off the whole area. No cars allowed." Buffy picked up an empty soda can and a fast-food wrapper and headed toward a curbside litter container.

"Too bad we can't put up a vamp blockade—*look out!*" Xander yelled.

Buffy jumped back as a truck loaded with heavy road barriers careened around the corner. An unstable stack of sawhorses fell off the truck onto the sidewalk where she had just been standing. Some of the wooden legs broke on impact and flew into the air. She caught a splintered piece of two-by-four before it hit her in the chest.

"Nice catch." Xander sagged, breathless from the close call.

"Instant stakes." Oz took the broken sawhorse leg from Buffy's hand and dropped it into the wire trash container. "Sunnydale attacks the Slayer. That's a twist."

Buffy glared at the truck as it sped on down the street, then glanced at Xander. "Thanks. For the warning, I mean."

"No problem." Xander frowned. "Funny thing, though."

Oz looked at him askance. "There's humor here?"

"No." Xander shook his head. "Funny because I knew those sawhorses were going to fall . . . *before* they fell."

"Weird, but fortunate for me." Buffy kicked at the pile of smashed barriers. "Guess we'll have to get someone to clean up the mess."

"Forget the mess. Don't you see?" Xander met Oz and Buffy's blank stares with shining eyes. "I *knew!*"

"Déjà vu." Oz began marking off the next display area. "It happens to everyone."

Buffy nodded.

"No, it was more than that," Xander insisted. "The danger was so clear. Like something *zapped* a message into my head!"

"Like psychic e-mail?" Buffy asked. "Or would that be p-mail?"

"That's it. Psychic!" Xander grinned, infused with sudden excitement. "There's no other explanation."

"Not necessarily." Oz glanced up. "Maybe you got a message from another Xander in the multiverse."

"From another who in the what?" Xander frowned.

"It's a scientific theory," Oz explained. "Some physicists believe that there are an infinite number of universes where all things that *can* happen *do* happen."

Buffy looked up from the box. "Meaning that in

one of these other universes I just got squashed by sawhorses?"

"Maybe." Oz nodded. "And since we're probably linked to our counterparts in these other universes, *that* Xander saw it happen and *our* Xander tuned in on it."

"So it *was* a psychic experience?" Xander asked Oz.

"Scientifically speaking. There's nothing supernatural about it." Oz reached for the masking tape, oblivious to the flicker of disappointment Buffy saw in Xander's eyes.

She had known for some time that Xander felt left out of the "extraordinary ability" loop. Even though he tackled whatever the Hellmouth threw at him, courage couldn't offset his strictly human status in his own mind. Having a Slayer, a witch, and a werewolf as best friends didn't help.

"Maybe I'm just a late bloomer in the paranormal scheme of things," Xander said, brightening. "It's possible, right?"

"In Sunnydale, *anything* is possible, Xander." Buffy saw no reason to bust his bubble.

Xander didn't say another word about the sawhorse incident as they blazed a masking tape trail down the block, but he couldn't stop thinking about it as he followed Oz and Buffy back to the gallery. Oz had rejected the idea that it might have been a psychic experience. That hurt, but not as much as being humored by the Slayer. Like he needed a paranormal bone to bolster his starved self-esteem.

Okay, so I do, Xander admitted to himself, but the image of falling sawhorses had been too clear to be dismissed as mere déjà vu. He had experienced the phenomenon of reliving some event or revisiting some place often enough to know that the sawhorse warning was different. The possibility that he might actually be psychic was a little hard to digest, but his friends' reactions had given him heartburn.

Why, Xander wondered, was it so hard for Buffy and Oz to even *consider* that he might have an emerging paranormal ability? Especially one that might be just as useful as casting spells or driving stakes through vampire hearts. *Just because I desperately* don't *want to be supernaturally impaired doesn't mean it can't happen!*

Willow looked up from the computer as they trooped into the gallery. "So—any action on the front lines?"

"Nope." Buffy sank into a second chair Willow had put behind the table. "But then, it isn't dark, yet."

"Buffy had a near miss with a sawhorse stampede, though." Oz dropped the supply box on the floor.

"Sawhorse?" Willow blinked. "One of those wooden two-by-four thingies? With—"

"—no head, no tail," Xander said simultaneously. His heart leaped. "There! It happened again."

"What?" Willow looked confused.

"I *knew* what you were going to say before you said it, Will," Xander explained.

"Not unusual," Oz said. "For someone who's known Willow since kindergarten."

"Maybe." Xander wasn't about to disregard the psychic implication just because Oz's logic made annoying sense. "But I've never met those sawhorses before in my life."

"They were . . . alive?" Willow frowned.

"No, but I saw them fall off the truck." Xander quickly clarified. *"Before* they self-destructed on the street."

"Like a . . . a premonition?" Willow asked.

"Something like that," Buffy said.

"Exactly like that." Xander tensed under Willow's skeptical scrutiny. She wasn't taking his psychic prospects seriously, either.

"Excuse me?" A soft feminine voice interrupted. "Is this where I check in for the art show?"

They all turned to the newcomer.

"Uh, yeah. This is the place." Xander marveled at his ability to speak with his heart lodged in his throat. The young woman's short raven black hair framed a cameo face dominated by the biggest, darkest eyes he had ever seen. Her pale skin was flawless, but since the sun was just setting and she wasn't smoking or ablaze, that vampire-like quality didn't set off any alarms.

"Except, well, artist registration doesn't start until tomorrow," Willow said.

"Oh, dear." The young artist's full lips puckered into a disappointed pout. "I was hoping to set up tonight so I could spend tomorrow finishing a couple of pieces."

"Maybe that could be arranged." Xander caught the girl's grateful glance and cast one of his own at Buffy. "If somebody with pull asks for a favor."

Buffy started. "Meaning me?"

"You've got more influence with your mom than I do," Xander said.

"I'd really appreciate it." The young woman smiled and extended her hand to Buffy. "Justine Camille."

"Buffy Summers." Buffy shook Justine's hand and gave Xander a sidelong scowl.

Xander deflected it with a shrug. He could handle some Slayer disapproval if it made points with the gorgeous artist.

"Your mom's in the office, Buffy." Willow waved toward the back of the gallery. "Actually, it might not be a bad idea. To let Justine sign in now, I mean. We'll be mobbed tomorrow, and well, I've only got one computer."

"Good point." Buffy jumped up. "Be right back."

"Just fill this out with your local contact info." Willow handed Justine a form.

Xander shifted awkwardly as the young woman walked by him without a glance. Then he realized he looked like Construction Guy in his tool belt and scruffy work clothes. *Not exactly the right boy bait to attract an elegant artistic type.* He was caught completely off guard when Justine suddenly flashed him a brilliant smile over her shoulder.

"Thanks so much—"

"Uh, Xander." Xander nodded. "Harris. You need anything, just ask."

"Excellent!" Justine hesitated, nibbling her lip. "I don't suppose you could help me unload my van?"

"Uh—I could." Xander kept nodding. "I mean, sure. Yes. Whenever you're ready."

That was so not slick. Xander perched on the edge of the table to wait, pretending to ignore Justine and hoping to recoup some semblance of cool. *As long as nobody mentions high school, I've got a shot with Justine for coffee. Or maybe even late night snack date—*

"Well! Looks like everyone's here." Cordelia Chase breezed into the gallery looking casually chic in black pants, boots and a sequined, blue top. Her hair was swept back and clipped in a cascade of dark curls.

Xander's mouth went dry as Cordy's glance swept across him and came to rest on his tool belt.

"Don't tell me." Cordy cocked her head. "You've finally settled on a career as a handyman?"

"Actually, I'm a member of the art show staff," Xander said. *No cracks. Just the facts,* he reminded himself when Justine glanced over her shoulder.

"So am I. Mrs. Summers asked me to be the publicity liaison for a VIP." Cordy scanned the gallery. "Is Buffy's mom here?"

"In her office." Xander thumbed toward the back and exhaled as Cordy left without a parting insult. He had gotten off easy.

By the time Buffy returned with Joyce's permission to let Justine check in, Willow was already entering the artist's contact information into the registration program.

"The Golden Lantern Motel is old—but nice," Willow observed as she typed. "And close, too. It's only a couple blocks from your display site—"

"Although I wouldn't recommend walking," Xander interjected. "Alone or after dark."

"Uh—right." Willow winced slightly and pulled Justine's site map from the printer. She highlighted the artist's display area. "Site number two-thirty-eight. On Main between Fourth and Vista."

"Got it." Xander eased off the table and gallantly gestured toward the door. He wanted to whisk Justine away before Cordelia finished her business with Joyce. "After you, Justine."

"Thanks for everything, Willow. You, too, Buffy." Flashing Xander another brilliant smile, Justine led the way to her van.

Xander slipped into the passenger side and pointed her in the right direction. "You've got a great location, Justine. Right in the middle of town. Lots of action—in a pedestrian sense. Customers, that is."

"I'm glad to hear that," Justine said. "I need some solid sales if I want to keep traveling the show circuit. A gallery show in New York or L.A. would be better, though. That's the only way an artist can build a reputation."

Out of his element on the topic of fine arts, Xander just nodded. "Do you need help setting up your display?"

Justine looked surprised. "I was just trying to decide if it would be presumptuous to ask you!"

"You were?" Xander cleared his throat, then bit his tongue. Justine needed muscle, but maybe that wasn't the sole source of her interest in him. He wasn't going to risk a total turn off by mentioning anything weird like psychic ability.

"This may sound strange, Xander, but . . . you exude an astonishing amount of psychic energy."

Xander stared at her open-mouthed. Apparently, his emerging ability to sense the future had endowed him with a powerful psychic presence, too. *Buffy's too close to me to feel it. As a stranger, Justine is more sensitive to my psychic vibes.* She also didn't know he had been power-challenged most of his life.

"I . . . don't talk about it much," Xander said.

"I understand." Justine's eyes sparkled as she studied him. "When we're done, would you let me do a Tarot reading? I don't find subjects with your . . . *qualities* very often."

"Telling the future with cards, right?" Xander's nonchalant shrug masked an inner turmoil. His friends' skepticism had shaken his confidence. A Tarot reading might prove his psychic talent was real and not just wishful thinking. He had to know.

Before the credibility gap becomes a canyon.

CHAPTER 3

"**S**o . . . this is the Golden Lantern Motel." Xander forced the words past the lump in his throat as he stopped in the doorway of Justine's room. He shoved his hands into his pocket and rocked back on his heels. *And I thought having my psychic thrusters activated was the high point in an otherwise ordinary week.*

"Come on in, Xander." Justine pulled a deck of cards from her bag and tossed the bag on the floor. "Do you want something to drink?"

"Drink?" Xander stared at the artist. Being alone with a beautiful woman in a motel room had put his brain into a synaptic stall. The snappy patter was on hold until his hormone levels leveled out. *Beautiful and talented,* he thought when he saw the four, unfinished paintings on the bed by the wall. The large, charcoal sketches depicted strange fantasy scenes. *Beautiful, talented, and weird, but not that bizarre by Sunnydale standards. I can deal.*

Justine reached into a cooler on the dresser. "I've got ginger ale, cola—"

"Ginger ale." Xander took the can from Justine and popped the top. "Thanks."

Justine flashed Xander another brilliant smile as she sat on the bed. "Shall we get started?"

Xander took a swallow and sputtered. The gods of geek-guys-who-might-get-lucky were with him, though, and soda didn't spray from his mouth. It just dribbled down his chin. "Started as in—"

Justine held up her Tarot deck.

"—Tarot reading. I'm ready whenever you are." Xander wasn't sure what he was supposed to do. "Is there some kind of ritual or something?"

She tucked her legs under her as she laughed. "Nothing special. It's all in the cards. Have a seat." She patted the bed.

"Right. Might as well be comfortable." Xander perched on the edge of the mattress, leaving room for the cards between him and the amused, young woman. In the back of his mind he was aware that he didn't have a clue what to expect. *What good is being psychic if it doesn't work when you need it?*

"Just relax, Xander," Justine said. "It's painless— unless you've got some deep, dark secret you don't want me to know."

Xander tensed. Justine was kidding, but he suddenly wondered just how much she could find out. Not that he had much to hide beyond rating a near zero in the high school stud pool even though he had stolen a kiss from Willow and lost Cordelia forever and spent most of his spare time almost getting killed by demons and vampires. *Nothing to worry about.*

"Touch the cards, Xander." Justine held out the deck and drew his gaze. "You have to transfer your psychic energy into the deck."

Xander hesitated. "My psychic energy? All of it?"

"No." Justine smiled. "Just a little so the reading will reflect your future."

"Oh, right." Xander wiped his sweating palm on his jeans and touched the deck. A tingling instantly affected his fingers and seemed to shoot directly to his brain. He swayed, suddenly dizzy.

"Are you okay?" Justine frowned as she pulled the deck back.

"Uh, yeah. It's been a long day." Xander shrugged, but couldn't shake the odd disconnect he felt with his own head. "Just a little tired, I guess."

"And tense. Relax."

The tension immediately drained from Xander's body and mind as Justine pulled the first card from the deck and placed it faceup on the bed.

"This card, the Knight of Swords, represents you, Xander," Justine explained.

"Is that cool?" Xander asked. "Being the Knight of Swords, I mean."

"That depends on the subject, but in your case—definitely." Justine drew a second card and put it faceup covering the first. "The Seven of Cups represents the circumstances surrounding you. Very interesting."

"How interesting?" Xander wasn't concerned, just curious.

"You're dealing with a lot of choices right now."

That's true, but hardly an earthshaking revelation, Xander thought. Everyone faced many choices every day. *But what to get when the bakery runs out of jelly doughnuts probably isn't on anyone else's critical-choice list.*

"You have dreams, but there's deception in your life, too, Xander," Justine went on. "And a sense of dissipation of self from within or from others."

Xander sighed. He had one dream—to work his way around the country unencumbered by school, parents, and a lifelong rep as a loser. And he wouldn't exactly mind a few months away from the demon denizens of Sunnydale, either. Although, he realized with a jolt, this was the first time he had actually admitted it to himself. The thought was disturbing, almost as disturbing as the deception and dissipation part. Sometimes he did feel like he had no substance, like he was just another stake in the Slayer's back pocket. Handy to have around, but not irreplaceable.

Where did that come from? Xander wondered and changed focus again.

"What deception?" Still feeling dizzy, Xander braced himself with his arm.

"Fooling yourself, perhaps?" Justine shrugged. "Or hiding things from the people around you who care? Only you know, Xander. And the cards, of course."

"I'm not liking this much so far," Xander said.

"Enlightenment is never easy, but once you achieve it, you'll never regret it." Justine placed a third card perpendicular over the first two.

"Death?" Apprehension gripped Xander when he read the title scripted below the image of the Grim Reaper. "Can we stop now?"

"It's symbolic," Justine said, "not literal. Whatever the Death card represents, it indicates transformation."

No! Xander reacted to the first thing that came to mind. *Not into a vampire!*

Justine didn't notice his apprehension and kept talking. "Generally speaking, the Death card deals with change that's based on the destruction of what already exists. Which isn't all bad," she hastily added. "Necessarily."

"It isn't?"

"The changes might be new opportunities you haven't been in a position to consider, yet. Something ends . . . something else begins. That kind of thing."

"Like graduation?" Xander flinched, remembering his desire to appear older to Justine. "As an example, I mean."

"Yes." Nodding her approval, Justine drew the fourth card. She placed it toward Xander separate from the three cards that were already on the bed. "The Three of Swords. You've had some trouble in your romantic affairs lately."

Xander didn't say anything. He stared at the picture of a heart impaled by three swords. The image perfectly described how he felt about the entire Cordelia—Willow episode. He hurt because he hadn't fallen for Willow until it was too late, but the pain he had inflicted on Cordelia was worse. He saw her again, lying in a heap under the broken warehouse stairs with a metal re-bar driven through her. He was ashamed at his behavior.

"I guess we touched a nerve, huh?" Justine asked softly.

"A few." Xander couldn't tear his eyes away from the pierced heart.

"Let's move on, then. Maybe it'll get better." Justine peeled another card off the deck and set it down to the left of the first three cards. "Then again, maybe not."

The Hermit? "What does that mean? That I'm destined to be a lonely old fool?"

Justine shook her head. "Not necessarily. The Hermit indicates that you don't want to grow up and you don't listen when people offer good advice. In fact, you've fooled yourself and everyone around you into thinking you're completely unconcerned about your life and fate when you're actually running away from reality."

Xander looked the artist in the eye. "I don't feel better."

Justine shrugged. "The first five cards represent present or past circumstances. Tarot only predicts the future that *might* be. People have free will. They can change their destinies if they want to."

"That's comforting, I guess," Xander mumbled.

Justine's eyes widened slightly when she turned over the sixth card and placed it over the first three cards. "Ah! This is encouraging."

The dark despair pressing in on Xander lifted under the artist's smile. "I'm afraid to ask."

"The High Priestess represents your most probable future. It's not set in stone, of course, but the perfect woman is part of your destiny." Justine paused, then looked up at him. "And it seems you may possess psychic ability as well."

"I knew it!" Xander grinned. "Finally."

"Finally?" Justine frowned, perplexed.

"Uh—nothing." Xander struggled to explain his outburst. He certainly couldn't tell her he was the odd man out among friends who all had supernatural ability. "I, uh—just always thought there was something, you know?"

"Oh, yes." Justine nodded and flicked her wrist to flash the Tarot deck. "I know."

Xander watched with anticipation as she dealt card number seven. His better mood vanished when she turned up the Hanged Man to the right of the center pile. "Please, tell me this doesn't mean what it looks like, either."

"It doesn't." Justine laughed. "How does wisdom

and prophetic power sound? And, perhaps, a span of time in the near future when you won't have to make any decisions."

"I'll take it." Euphoria seemed to cloud Xander's head for a moment. Not surprising given the portent of the Tarot reading, he realized. For the past three years he had been the ordinary sidekick to the Slayer and all-around errand boy. Now, at last, he had a paranormal ability he could use to help defeat the Sunnydale demon infestation. "Deal again."

Justine turned over the Wheel of Fortune and placed it to the right of the Hanged Man. "And what you fear."

Xander nodded and waited. If the card didn't indicate that his worst fears centered on the legions of undead and other atrocities the Hellmouth spewed out, he wasn't going to tell Justine. She might pack up and leave.

"You're a classic Peter Pan personality type, Xander." Justine smiled. "Not in a hurry to accept adult responsibility or to change."

"And lose my boyish charm?" Xander joked, but he didn't miss the point. Fate had endowed Buffy with a mission in life as the Slayer. Oz was totally dedicated to his music in spite of his monthly lapses into lupine ferocity, and Willow was determined to develop her magickal powers for good. He wasn't driven by anything except being accepted as an equal by his friends. *Which* was *a joke until my psy-*

chic powers came out of the closet today, Xander thought. *Now that I have something extraordinary to contribute, everything will change.*

But Justine didn't need to know that, either.

"Change is inevitable," Justine said. "Perhaps, sooner than you think."

"You have no idea." Xander noted the young woman's coy smile and had to still a racing heart again. He didn't know anything about Tarot, but Justine's reading had been remarkably accurate. Was it possible she used her skills to get to know the men *inside* the bods she found attractive?

"The ninth card reveals how your family and friends perceive you." Justine placed the next card above the Wheel of Fortune.

"The Fool? My friends think I'm a fool?" Xander glared at the image of a court jester.

"Foolish in a worldly sense," Justine explained. "You're a dreamer and, well—your friends and family think they have a better grip on reality than you do."

Justine quickly went on to reveal the Magician, which she put above the Fool. "There is hope for you, though. You will achieve mastery over something and with it, you'll be able to direct great power."

Suddenly spooked, Xander looked up. If he could fine-tune his psychic talent to accurately predict events, he *would* be using it to direct power. He'd be telling the Slayer what would happen, when and where!

"And finally—" Justine tensed a bit as she turned over the last card and set it down above the Magician. "The Nine of Pentacles. Excellent."

"It is?" Xander held his breath.

Justine nodded. "In the end, you'll be wise enough to know where your interest lies and what to do about it. You'll resolve the dilemma you were struggling with when we started."

Xander wasn't aware of any dilemma except wondering whether to risk shattering his fragile ego by asking Justine to go out. He seized the moment. "Want to go for coffee—or something to eat? The Bronze is loud, but they make a great cappuccino."

Justine held him transfixed with liquid brown eyes. "You're too tired, aren't you?"

Xander's eyelids drooped. "No, not really," he lied as exhaustion threatened to knock him out on the spot.

Justine stood up, pulled Xander to his feet, and guided him to the door. "Go home and get some rest. I'll see you at the art show tomorrow."

"Right. It must be later than I realized." Xander stumbled outside and dragged himself home. He got up the front steps without breaking his neck and collapsed on the worn sofa. He couldn't stay awake long enough to make it to his bedroom.

CHAPTER 4

Giles set his book and tea aside as Buffy, Willow, and Oz barged into the Sunnydale High library.

"Giles!" Buffy stuck her head in the office door. "Busy?"

"Actually, no," Giles said dryly. Although he still advised Buffy, he had much less paperwork to do since his separation from the Watchers Council. Sorting and shelving school library books demanded a hard ten minutes a day, since they were rarely checked out.

"You're sure?" Buffy's glance locked on the book as Giles marked his place. "I mean, you're reading."

"Librarians do that on occasion." Giles rose and picked up his tea.

"So whatever it is, it's nothing I should wonder

about?" Buffy asked as she followed him to the large study table.

"Not unless you've recently developed an interest in the works of Charles Dickens," Giles quipped.

"Don't think so." Buffy frowned. "Didn't he write 'The Christmas Song'?"

"Mel Torme." Oz dropped into a chair and propped his feet on the table. Giles casually swept them off as he walked by.

"Dickens wrote *A Christmas Carol*." Willow sat down beside Oz. "You know . . . the dastardly Scrooge goes tripping through time with the spirits of Christmas past, present and future?"

"Oh, yeah!" Buffy brightened. "Great movie—for black and white."

Shaking his head, Giles glanced toward the door as Xander rushed in.

"Sorry I'm late. Overslept." Xander darted into the office. He emerged again scowling. "I sleep in one lousy morning and no one else can get the doughnuts?"

Oz looked up. "Didn't think of it."

"Which is too bad because I'm kind of hungry, too," Willow said.

"Maybe we should kick the doughnut habit now anyway." Buffy shrugged as all eyes turned to stare. "Before they pass the fat tax."

"Are you all just looking for a handout or is there some sort of emergency?" Giles asked.

"More like emergency control." Buffy perched on

the edge of the study table. "Mom wants Slayer security at the art festival this weekend."

"The whole town is smitten with normalcy because of the art show," Willow said. "Nobody thought about the PR problems if, well—we have to be realistic, right? If the local vampires pig out and a bunch of artists end up dead—"

"Or undead," Oz inserted.

"Mom will feel responsible," Buffy finished.

"Yes, she would," Giles agreed.

"Which is why I want to know if something other than the usual horde of fanged guys is planning to pop out of the Hellmouth," Buffy said.

"Yes, well . . . that, uh . . . would be rather disruptive." Giles pulled a handkerchief from his pocket and wiped his glasses.

"I'm not picking up any weird vibes." Xander sat on the stairs and stretched.

Giles looked up, squinted. "A post-shock tremor?"

Buffy shook her head. "That's aftershock, but Xander's not talking earthquake."

"He thinks he's psychic—" Willow recoiled when Xander's head snapped up. "And, well . . . maybe he is . . . maybe."

"Do tell." Replacing his glasses, Giles paused to absorb Willow's comment about Xander's prognostication potential. His initial reaction was a silent, but unequivocal "unlikely."

"I don't just think, I *know*," Xander insisted. "But obviously, everyone else finds it a little hard to believe. Why? Nobody has a problem with Buffy being the legendary vampire Slayer or Willow making mojo or Oz turning into Dog Man."

"Yes, but the evidence regarding Buffy, Willow, and Oz's . . . *unique* abilities is beyond dispute," Giles said. "Did you experience a psychic episode?"

"Yes." Xander sat back, arms folded, and launched into a detailed account of yesterday's events. Giles listened attentively, but was not swayed by what amounted to Xander's impassioned desire to join the ranks of the extraordinary.

"But last night was proof positive." Xander hesitated, his eyes glazing for an instant. When he resumed speaking, he seemed distant and subdued, a jolting switch from his previously impassioned tone. "I didn't say a *word* to Justine about being psychic, but she picked up on it right away."

"Excuse me?" Giles blinked. "Who's Justine?"

"One of the artists," Buffy explained. "A charming, *pretty* artist to be exact."

"She isn't just an artist." Xander leaned forward. "After we set up her display, we went back to her motel—"

"For a romantic interlude?" Willow asked with an impish smile.

"Tarot reading," Xander said. "According to Justine, I radiate psychic energy like a furnace blasts hot air."

"No other similarity implied." The corner of Oz's mouth twitched, but he didn't smile.

"Psychic energy isn't the same thing as psychic

ability," Giles explained. He didn't want to damage Xander's fragile ego, but he couldn't let the mistaken assumption pass. "Everyone exudes a certain amount of psychic energy—like a psychic signature, which is transferred into the Tarot deck by touching the cards. Thus, each deal is specific to the individual subject."

Xander's brow furrowed over a fleeting, almost vacant stare.

"Is Tarot reliable?" Buffy scowled, looked at Giles. "Or just complicated fortune cookies?"

"That depends on the expertise of the person doing the reading. The cards *can* evoke intellectual and emotional insight from the inner consciousness of an astute reader. To others, it's nothing more than an amusing parlor game." Giles refrained from pointing out that Justine might be simply enamored of the occult and an untrained dabbler.

"So good Tarot takes the guesswork out of destiny?" Buffy asked.

"Not exactly," Willow said, brushing her auburn hair behind her ear. "It doesn't foretell the future. A reading just gives hints of what could be or might be."

"Indications," Giles agreed. "Tarot is used as a tool of enlightenment designed to help people understand themselves and their relationship with the cosmos. Internal rather than external in nature."

Willow brightened suddenly. "Maybe you should get a reading done, Buffy! It might help you pick a career."

"No thanks." Buffy shook her head. "My destiny is set in stone."

"Well, the future of *my* internal nature includes psychic abilities." Xander returned to a defensive posture when he drew everyone's gaze. "The High Priestess said so."

"Justine's a high priestess, too?" Buffy's eyes widened. "Of what cult?"

Giles smiled. "The High Priestess is a card, Buffy. One of the original twenty-two cards in ancient Tarot decks. It's believed that all earthly emotions and experiences are revealed through the Major Arcana."

Willow looked at Xander. "So the High Priestess must have been your crown card."

"Beats me." Xander shifted. "There were a lot of cards. I don't remember all the details."

"Yes, well—the High Priestess as a crown card might also indicate that unknown, hidden forces are at work in your future, Xander." Giles shrugged. "Rather than psychic ability."

Xander's eyes flashed with challenge. "The hanged guy. Near future. Symbolic of prophetic *power.*"

Buffy and Willow exchanged a glance, startled by Xander's display of temper.

"Or stagnation," Giles countered, keeping his tone even. Xander's angry desperation was unsettling, but he knew that being honest with the boy now might avert more bitter disappointment later. "Every card has a positive and negative meaning."

"So naturally, it's not even remotely possible for

yours truly to be positively psychic." Xander shook his head, then stood up and headed for the large double doors of the library.

"Xander, wait—" Willow started to rise.

"What for?" Xander's jaw flexed as he spun to face them. "You guys haven't finished pounding me to a psychological pulp yet? Forget it. I'm gone."

"But—" Willow sat back down as Xander stormed out, the doors swinging shut behind him.

Giles flinched, then sighed. "It would seem I muddled that rather too well."

"Not your fault, Giles." Buffy's gaze lingered on the doors. "Xander's always had a no-power complex. He'll get over it."

"But what if he doesn't?" Willow sagged. "I've never seen him so . . . so—"

"Crushed?" Oz offered.

"Shredded." Willow sagged.

Buffy turned her worried gaze on Giles. "Any chance Xander really has suddenly tuned in to the cosmic pipeline?"

"Possible, perhaps, but I rather suspect he's simply experiencing normal bursts of intuition," Giles said.

"Then how did he know the sawhorses would fall off the truck?" Buffy asked.

"Easily explained, actually," Giles said. "The stack of sawhorses may have wobbled as the truck began to turn the corner. Xander's mind processed that observable information so quickly he wasn't aware of it. Consequently, it seemed like a flash of psychic insight."

"I've had that happen," Oz said. "It's like 'something' tells you not to follow the car ahead too close, and then a few seconds later it blows out a tire."

"So what should we do?" Buffy slid off the table and nodded toward the doors. "About Xander."

"Nothing." Giles wasn't a psychologist, but he was fairly certain Xander's anger would pass when he calmed down enough to think rationally. "If we're wrong, we'll have ample opportunity to beg for his forgiveness after he demonstrates a psychic talent beyond normal parameters. However, since I doubt that will happen, I see no reason to press him about his folly."

Willow frowned. "I wonder if the Fool card showed up in his reading."

Xander's anger subsided before he hit the courtyard. He sank onto a stone bench and closed his eyes, his thoughts focused on what he hadn't told his friends about the Tarot reading. Justine had been absolutely certain about his psychic powers, but the cards had revealed other, less positive things about him and his future, too. He didn't remember the details, but the general gist was hard to forget.

A loser in love, he was deluding himself, resisting change, and running away from reality.

"You're a classic Peter Pan personality . . ." Justine had laughed when she said it, but the words had struck an uncomfortable chord.

"And she knows I'm unlucky in love," Xander muttered. The dismal prospect of his un-social life was troubling—file that idea under run-for-your-life—but not as devastating as his friends' tolerant, patronizing perceptions of him.

While most of the cards had become a blur, the Fool card mocked him with disturbing clarity. The jester represented the opinion of his peers, and Justine had not pulled the punch. His friends thought he was a foolish, ignorant dreamer.

Last night he had scoffed at the idea.

This morning Buffy, Willow, Oz, and Giles had all proved it was true.

Xander opened his eyes, exhaled, and stared at the cracks in the cement walkway. The clear image of the Fool began to fade.

When he looked up again, he was walking down a residential street—with no recollection of how he had gotten there.

CHAPTER 5

As the last artist hurried out the gallery door, Willow sighed with relief. She had gone straight to the art show headquarters after school to relieve the only volunteer Joyce had found for temporary registration duty. Except for a break to grab a soda from the office fridge and stretch, she had been anchored in front of the computer for hours. Most of the artists had registered by early evening, but others were still straggling in.

"Hey, Will!" Buffy entered as Willow started toward the office. "How's it going?"

"Okay." Willow wiggled her fingers. "I haven't developed stiff knuckles from typing. Yet. Where's Oz?"

"Still setting up. Some of these people won't finish until midnight." Buffy sighed and zipped into the office ahead of her. "Want a soda?"

Willow nodded and took the cold can Buffy offered. "Have you seen Xander?"

"He's been helping the artists, too." Buffy popped the top on her can and leaned against the desk. "In between very long breaks hanging out at Justine's display."

"I guess he's still mad, huh?" Willow hadn't meant to hurt Xander's feelings that morning—none of them had—but he was taking it hard. When he had finally checked into the gallery, he had barely spoken. *If grunts and monosyllables count as talking,* she thought with dismay.

"Or he just needs a little space to lick his wounds. I tried to smooth things over, but he didn't have much to say. Too embarrassed about the psychic thing maybe." Buffy reached for the Slayer bag on the floor and pulled out a stake.

"Probably, but Xander on a verbal strike is . . . creepy." Willow shuddered.

"Definitely. I hope he snaps out of it soon." Buffy slid the stake into her back pocket and paused on her way out the door. "Sun's setting and I don't want to keep Angel waiting."

"Tell Oz I'll see him later." As Willow wandered back to the computer, she suspected Buffy was more worried about Xander than she sounded. The Slayer just didn't know what to do about it, either.

"Willow! Is Xander here?" Anya strode toward the registration table.

"No, he's out there somewhere." Willow waved toward the door. "Helping—uh—the artists set up their stuff . . . and stuff."

"Oh." Anya stared at Willow, her jaw set. "Well, let me ask you something."

Willow eyed her warily. "What?"

"How do I get a guy?"

Disarmed by Anya's question, Willow experienced a momentary brain fumble. "Get a guy what?"

"To like me. If I were interested in one—hypothetically—and he ignored me." Anya scowled. "What would I do about it?"

"I'm not the person to ask, Anya."

Anya rolled her eyes. "You're a human female so you have inherent instincts on how to attract men. There must be some learned techniques women use in these situations."

Willow almost smiled at the irony. Anya had spent the past millennium avenging scorned women by punishing and repelling men. Now that she was stuck in a teenaged, female body, all she seemed to think about was snaring "a boy"—most likely Xander.

"It's been so long since I was human, I've forgotten what works and what doesn't." Anya's frown deepened. "If I ever knew. Social standards were a lot different during the Dark Ages."

"Oh, well—yeah." Willow didn't know how to respond. She still wasn't comfortable with the ex-demon and didn't trust her. *Even if I was an expert on how to lure a guy, which I'm not, why should I help her?*

"So?" Anya prodded her.

Willow shook her head. She knew from experience that Anya wouldn't just drop the subject and go away—not empty-handed anyway. She was as stubborn as she was blunt. Besides, nothing Anya did would change Xander's mind about her unless he honestly wanted to be swayed. Which he probably didn't now that he had Justine. For the weekend anyway.

"Um . . . what about . . . Well, you could try to make him jealous," Willow suggested. That wasn't her style and it probably wouldn't work, but she had to offer Anya something.

"Jealous?" Anya brightened, then frowned again. "I should have thought of that. I've been driving men mad with jealousy for centuries."

"It does seem to work. People don't know what they've got until they don't have it anymore." Willow smiled. "If Xander—I mean, this hypothetical guy—thinks you've got someone else then maybe he'll be sorry he didn't pay more attention to you . . . when he had the chance."

"Okay." Anya had no compunction about using deception as a means to an end. "Where do I get someone else in a hurry?"

"You could try the Bronze." Willow didn't have a clue, but she couldn't solve all of Anya's problems.

As if on cue, though, she looked past Anya just in

time to see a tall, handsome young man in a sports jacket and jeans walk in. He had a camera slung over his shoulder and a small computer notebook in his hand. "Can I help you?"

"Rob Chambers, *California Art* magazine." He smiled at Willow, then Anya.

"You'll do." Anya stood back, unabashed as her gaze flicked from the mop of curly, dark hair that crowned his tanned face to his casual loafers. "Let's go out. Now."

Anya's direct approach took Willow by surprise. She kept expecting the ex-demon to develop some basic social skills.

Rob recovered easily. "I'd love to, but I'm on assignment covering the show. Is Cordelia Chase here?"

"Not at the moment, but she will be." Willow glanced toward the door. In a mutually beneficial arrangement that would both pad her college application as well as boost PR for the gallery and next year's Sidewalk Art Festival, Cordelia had offered to take charge of the reporter. Cordelia's style and attitude were perfect for the job. *Not to mention that her vampire awareness will help keep Mr. Chambers alive long enough to write a review.*

As though on cue, Cordelia made her grand entrance. Wearing a black skirt and fitted, black jacket over a sea-green blouse and spiked heels, she was the epitome of elegance. She flashed a perfect smile. "Mr. Chambers?"

"Yes—" Only Rob's eyes betrayed his appreciation of Cordelia's stunning beauty as he turned. "Ms. Chase?"

"Cordelia, please. Sorry I'm late, but there's no parking anywhere with all these artists jamming the streets." Cordy glanced at Willow. "Are we going to have to deal with that inconvenience all weekend?"

Willow shrugged. "Traffic control isn't my department."

"Not a problem, I assure you." Rob gripped Cordy's hand firmly for several seconds longer than necessary. "I rather enjoy evening strolls with beautiful women."

"You've never been to Sunnydale before," Anya said dryly.

Willow nudged her. *A message she may or may not get,* she thought with a fixed smile. She needn't have worried. Rob was too enthralled with Cordelia to notice.

"Then a walking tour seems like a good way to begin." Cordy linked her arm through Rob's and steered him toward the door.

"Where are you going?" Willow asked when Anya moved to follow.

"I need another man if I'm going to make Xan—*anyone* jealous." Anya spoke without looking back.

Willow just shook her head. Anya was zeroed in on Xander like a heat-seeking missile on an active volcano.

Anya paused on the sidewalk to watch as Cordelia and Rob stopped to speak to an artist unloading a covered pickup truck. *Is she admiring his work or blasting him for taking her parking spot?* Anya wondered as an aside. Her attention was on the reporter.

He was attractive in a casual, rugged way, but looking at him didn't make the hair on her neck tingle or tighten her stomach with longing. Just *thinking* about Xander made her feel awful. Rob would be a poor substitute, but then she wasn't looking for love. She just needed a relatively attractive, male presence to raise the green-eyed monster of envy in Xander.

"Nothing to lose and Xander to gain," Anya said as Rob and Cordelia moved on. Her plan to entice the young man away from Xander's ex-girlfriend was simple. Cordelia was being coy. Anya didn't have the patience to play games. Her experience as Anyanka had taught her one thing well: *Men aren't all that patient, either.*

Anya wove her way through knots of people who were putting together their display areas. She had never been to a modern art show, but she assumed the craft people would display their wares for sale tomorrow. *Kind of like the European village vendors a few centuries ago,* she thought. *Reminds me of the time I turned an unfaithful copper tinker into a tavern wench—with entertaining results.*

As Anya closed in, Rob paused to survey the scene and typed a few notes into his electronic notebook. He smiled at Cordelia. "As long as we're out here, I'd like to talk to some of the artists. Get some of their backgrounds—"

"Whatever you want." Cordelia beamed back. "When you're finished, would you be interested in checking out the local night life? It's kinda dead, but the Bronze makes a fabulous double-mocha coffee."

"Sounds like a 'must-do' to me." Rod placed his hand on Cordy's back to ease her around a large toolbox on the sidewalk.

Rolling her eyes, Anya quickened her pace to catch up and came to an abrupt halt when Rob and Cordelia stopped by a nearly completed display. Xander sat on a chair in the center of the U-shaped panels. A too-pretty, young female artist was hanging her paintings and glanced at Rob and Cordelia curiously. Xander stared at his feet.

"The show doesn't open until tomorrow," the artist said.

"I'm Rob Chambers, a reporter for *California Art* magazine." Rob stepped closer to study the paintings. "These are excellent—for fantasy."

"Justine Camille. You don't like fantasy, Mr. Chambers?" The artist followed Rob and Cordelia as they moved from one piece to another.

Anya planted herself in front of Xander. "Hello, Xander."

Xander grunted in reply, but he didn't look at her.

"What are you doing?" Anya asked.

"Helping." Xander's gaze flicked to her face for a second, then fastened on the artist.

Anya felt as though he had just driven a stake through her human heart. She had learned to deal with being ignored and insulted, but not with Xander's interest in someone else. Anya's attention snapped to the dark-haired woman. Confused and hurt, she kicked his foot.

"What?" Xander frowned and tucked his feet under the chair. His annoyed glance immediately shifted back to Justine.

Anya was devastated and completely at a loss. The jealousy ploy only worked if the other person cared. Xander couldn't care less. "I don't like you anymore, Xander."

"Good." Xander's gaze remained on Justine.

"Believe me, Mr. Chambers," Justine was saying. "I will have a one-woman show at a major New York gallery within six months."

"I commend your ambition, but your expectations are unrealistic, Justine," Rob countered. "Fairies, dragons, and unicorns, no matter how well the pieces are executed, are only illustrations."

Anya stepped up beside Rob for a closer look at the paintings. The colorful, detailed depictions of make-believe creatures had a certain charm. More importantly, her work was Justine's weak spot and the perfect target for Anya's vengeance.

"I'm going to change that," Justine said with confidence.

"Fine art *is* Rob's business," Cordelia said. "I wouldn't take his advice lightly, Ms. Camille."

"Fantasy is a genre that will never be taken seriously by the fine-art world," Rob explained with a hint of exasperation.

"Then why are you wasting your time with *her*, Mr. Chambers?" Anya cast a scathing look at Justine and turned to leave.

"You'll be sorry for that," the artist whispered as Anya passed by.

The hollow threat fell on deaf ears. When Xander turned, his brooding stare bore through Anya, as though she wasn't even there.

Buffy heard the rattle of a trashcan in the dark alley behind her at the same time her Slayer sense detected the vampires. She didn't have to look to know Angel had swung to the left to flank the fanged stalkers. They were both ready for action after patrolling the art show perimeter for hours guarding the artists and volunteers from shadows and a few stray cats.

Buffy whipped the stake from her back pocket as she turned toward the alley. "Want to party?"

The first vamp burst from the dark corridor roaring. The large male was wearing a UC Sunnydale sweatshirt and was obviously driven by hunger rather than brains. He ran right into Buffy's raised stake in a desperate effort to grab her in a bear hug.

"Didn't study for your vampire midterms, huh?" Buffy quipped as he vanished in a cloud of dust.

The second was female and older. When her companion disintegrated, she turned and ran.

Angel darted from a doorway to intercept. Startled, the vamp tripped and self-destructed on a broken, wooden chair leg someone had discarded.

"That wasn't exactly a challenge," Buffy huffed.

Angel nodded with a thoughtful frown.

"What?" Buffy asked, pocketing her stake. The brooding look that haunted Angel's eyes was more intense than usual.

"It's too quiet," Angel said.

"Yeah, it is." Buffy glanced toward the street. One of the visiting artisans slammed his van doors closed. The middle-aged man didn't have a clue he was easy prey for Sunnydale's darker element. The undead were alarmingly absent, however. "Is something up we don't know about?"

"Not that I've heard, but . . ." Angel hesitated, his senses tuned to the nuances of evil that wafted through the night.

"Please, don't tell me you've got a bad feeling about this." Buffy's flip remark masked a shudder.

"I've got a bad feeling about . . . something." The vampire's human brow furrowed. "Willy might know."

"It's worth checking out," Buffy agreed. "Just in case." Willy ran the local demon watering hole and served as a handy Slayer snitch when proper pressure was applied.

"I'll call Giles, if I find out anything." Angel touched Buffy's shoulder and brushed her mouth with a hurried kiss before he vanished down the alley.

I'm in love with a shadow, Buffy thought, honing in on the dark silence that had absorbed the vampire. She didn't sense anything threatening, but some unidentified thingy had disturbed Angel. That was enough to make her wary.

With Sunnydale secure, Buffy headed back toward the gallery. Mayor Wilkins had dispatched extra police patrols as a precaution during the art show. They seemed to be more concerned with directing traffic and writing parking tickets than protecting the public, though. Still, the increased number of officers working the streets might have discouraged vampire gluttony. The average vamp tended to hunt alone and avoided conflict or complications.

When Buffy saw Xander walking on the far side of the street with Justine, she made a point of intercepting them. "Hi, Xander. How's it going?"

"Fine." Xander nodded, but without enthusiasm.

"How about some downtime at the Bronze?" Buffy suggested, suddenly feeling awkward. She hadn't realized just how deeply he had been hurt and she was at a loss what to do. "You, me, Oz, and Willow. Justine, too. If you want."

"Thanks, but I'm kind of tired." Justine smiled, but seemed ill at ease.

Tired or nervous? Buffy wondered as the artist took Xander's arm. *Probably both.* It had been an exhausting day for the artist, too, and her livelihood depended on selling her work over the weekend.

"Xander's walking me to my van." Justine pointed to a green van parked a short distance away.

"Good idea." Buffy noted the dragon painted on the side door. "I can wait."

"No, that's okay," Xander said.

Buffy frowned, but didn't argue. "Then maybe we'll see you later? We need to talk."

"Right." Xander sighed. "Later at the Bronze."

Worried, Buffy navigated her way through the artists finishing up their displays. She had never seen Xander so down. Willow knew Xander better than anyone. Maybe she had a clue how to set things right.

Buffy glanced toward the entrance again looking for Xander. Willow and Oz had met her at the Bronze over an hour ago and they had finally agreed to accept Giles's advice for a while longer.

"I'm not sure it's a perfect plan." Willow pushed her soda away. "But pushing Xander about being psychic might just drive him even farther away."

"Apparently, we've already driven him to emotional Outer Mongolia," Oz observed.

"What I was thinking," Buffy said. "Just not in those exact words." She frowned, her anxiety mounting about Xander's retreat into stubborn silence. His no-show at the Bronze was troubling, too. "Where is he, anyway?"

"Maybe he went home to sulk some more." Willow shrugged. "We were kind of hard on him this morning."

"Or maybe he's with Justine at her motel again," Oz said. "She had an exclusive on Xander's hammer and his company all day."

"And all night?" Buffy started to rise. "Maybe I'd better check."

"Not a good idea." Oz put a staying hand on Buffy's arm.

"Why not?" Buffy asked.

"The male–female equation for one thing," Oz explained. "Might be embarrassing."

Willow's eyes widened. "Especially for Xander. I mean, if Xander and Justine are together and you barge in to rescue him, it would kind of . . . kill the mood."

"And his image," Oz added.

"Oh, yeah. I didn't think of *that*. The boy–girl angle, I mean." Buffy sat back down, but she couldn't shake her unease. "So you guys don't think there's anything off about Justine?"

"Well, I suppose she could just be using Xander to help her with her art stuff," Willow said. "Or she might really like him."

Buffy nodded. "Okay, but Xander's romantic track record isn't all that great. He tends to attract assorted creatures of the night—and Cordelia—so my spidery-senses are up."

"Well, there's also the Tarot reading," Willow added. "And the psychic thing."

"Which Xander desperately wants to believe." The psychic angle made a little more sense, but it didn't calm Buffy's anxiety. "I'm still worried."

"I'll go." Oz squeezed Willow's shoulder and stood up. "I'm a guy. If I barge into a romantic clutch, it'll give Xander a macho boost."

Willow smiled. "According to her registration ticket, she's staying at the Golden Lantern."

"Justine drives a green van with a dragon on the door," Buffy said. "We'll wait here. Call us when you find him, okay?"

"Will do." Oz kissed Willow's cheek and nodded at Buffy as he left.

Buffy's smile faded as Oz disappeared into the crowd.

"Oz can handle it, Buffy," Willow assured her.

"I know, but can we handle *this?*" Buffy braced herself as Cordelia approached with an attractive man she dimly recognized from the festival grounds.

"Uh-oh." Willow winced.

"That had an ominous ring." Buffy gave Willow a sidelong glance, then followed her gaze past Cordelia. On the far side of the room, Anya slipped out of a booth and stormed toward them.

"Well, if things get interesting, it's all my fault," Willow muttered. "Anya came to me for advice on how to get Xander—well, hypothetical Xander, anyway—to notice her."

Buffy blinked. "So now we're Anya's support group?"

"I'm not happy about it." Willow sighed. "But I sort of suggested she could try making Xander jealous."

Buffy blinked again. "With Cordelia's date?"

"Reporter," Willow clarified. "He was the only guy in the gallery at the time. Anya asked. He turned her down to hang with Cordelia. Does that qualify as being scorned?"

Never a dull moment, Buffy thought as Cordy paused to introduce the reporter.

"Buffy Summers, this is Rob Chambers. He's covering the festival for an art magazine," Cordelia said. "Buffy's mom is running the art show."

"My pleasure, Buffy." Rob extended his hand. "I haven't met your mother—"

Anya didn't wait for a suitable break in the conversation or bother with opening pleasantries. "Where's Xander?"

"Don't know," Buffy answered. "Not here."

"Is he with that woman?" Anya interrupted.

Willow shrugged.

"If I had my powers I could turn her into an old hag, Willow. But maybe with your help we could conjure the next best thing?" Anya said with a hint of desperation.

Rob did a double take.

Buffy shook his hand. "Welcome to Sunnydale."

CHAPTER 6

Oz had no trouble locating Justine's room at the Gold Lantern Motel, an old, one-story structure. The green van with its distinctive dragon logo was parked outside the unit on the far end. Like Buffy, he was concerned about Xander's withdrawal, but he also understood that Xander's self-image was more vulnerable than usual.

So he probably won't appreciate me checking up on him, either, Oz thought as he walked across the pavement. Opting for discretion rather than a frontal assault, he peered in the window instead of knocking on the door. The curtain was open, giving him a view of most of the room.

Four large paintings stood propped against the far wall. All were fantasy images, but only one, which looked vaguely like the Grim Reaper, appeared to be finished.

There was no sign of Xander or—

"What are you doing?" a sharp, female voice demanded.

Oz managed to keep from jumping up. Instead, he turned slowly to face Justine. "Looking for Xander, actually. No one answered the door."

"I was at the vending machine in the office." She squinted at him, not sure she recognized him.

"Oz. We met at the gallery last night."

"Oh, yes." Justine tucked several packages under one arm and reached into a large cargo pants pocket with her free hand, presumably for her keys. "Xander went home over an hour ago."

Not to the Bronze, Oz noted with dismay. Xander's ego meltdown was worse than he had realized.

"Thanks. I'll check there." Oz accidentally jostled Justine's arm as he passed and two of the packages fell to the ground. He and the artist both stooped to pick them up, but his fingers closed on a deck of cards.

A sizzling tingle rushed from his hand into the deck. Startled, Oz stood up. A wave of dizziness overwhelmed him and he fell back against the wall. He blinked to clear his head, but everything seemed fuzzy. For a moment, he couldn't remember where he was.

Justine opened the door and stood back. "Come on in, Oz."

Oz swayed slightly. His entire awareness was suddenly focused on the calm, compelling sound of Justine's voice.

"Inside, Oz."

He wanted to refuse.

He walked into the room against his will.

Xander stared through a fog at the distorted images of the dream. Except it wasn't a dream—exactly. He *felt* like he was wandering through a barren terrain strewn with bones and punctuated by leafless trees, but he couldn't be. He was sure he was still lying on the old sofa in the basement, where he had been since Justine had told him to go home.

Am I asleep or awake?

Xander couldn't tell. He felt like he hadn't completely come out of the trance he had experienced during the Tarot reading the night before, which he hadn't mentioned to Giles or his friends.

Because Justine told me not to.

The realization that Justine had some kind of control over his actions today jarred him, but not hard enough to jolt him out of the nightmare.

Feathers fell from a vulture circling overhead. Xander ducked, only to be confronted by the robed Grim Reaper figure walking toward him out of a turbulent mist.

Just like the Death card painting in Justine's motel room.

Xander's displaced mind reeled as he recalled more details of the reading Justine had tried to block.

The Death card represented the past, the future, and change, a key factor in his reading according to Justine.

"The Death card deals with change that's based on the destruction of what already exists."

At the time, he had accepted Justine's assurances that that wasn't necessarily bad. Now, disoriented and confused, he wasn't so sure.

So what did Justine mean exactly? Xander wondered. Most people would address the portent metaphorically. *But then most people don't live on the Hellmouth.* He could be facing his own destruction, the destruction of everyone he cared about, or the end of the world. Not a unique scenario, but it never lacked for punch.

The world that was slowly superimposing itself over his family's basement seemed to support the destruction-of-the-world theory. The bleak landscape was, Xander realized, possibly his perception of death and annihilation—in progress!

Reacting to a hissing sound, he jumped as putrid gases spewed from the ground by his feet.

Except that he hadn't *actually* jumped. He was still lying on the sofa. He could see the television set through the wall of flame that erupted along the desert horizon. The bizarre nature of his circumstances became clear in an instant of horror. He was physically in one place and mentally in another.

Mist vaporized into sizzling steam as the black countenance under the Grim Reaper's hooded cloak bore down on him. Staring Death in the face made certain truths Xander had hidden from himself very clear, too.

He wasn't psychic. Disappointing, but not a tragedy. He had latched onto the possibility like a crutch to prop up his misguided sense of worthless self. His friends accepted and respected him for what he was—an ordinary guy who was always there and did his best no matter what. He could deal with that.

There's just one really big problem, Xander thought as the Death figure loomed over him and the fog cleared off a surreal landscape of jagged stone and cracked desert.

His mind was trapped in a Tarot card painting with no way out.

Willow shifted position on the barstool and checked the time. She and Buffy had moved to the counter after Cordelia and Rob had retreated to a private corner and Anya had departed to stake out Xander's house. They didn't want to miss Oz's phone call, but she was getting more and more nervous as the minutes ticked by with no word.

"Do you think something's wrong, Buffy? It's been almost an hour. I mean, I know Oz can look out for himself because of the wolf thing and all . . . but I'm a little worried."

"Me, too, but maybe that's just because Xander's been acting so weird." Buffy stopped drumming her fingers on the counter and straightened with resolve. "If we don't hear from Oz in the next five minutes, I'm out of here."

Willow nodded, but her anxiety didn't lessen. *What if something happened and Buffy's too late? Or what if he hasn't called because he hasn't found Xander—yet. . . .*

The phone at the far end of the bar rang.

"Finally," Buffy said when the bartender waved Willow over.

Willow was already off her stool and taking the phone. "Oz! Is everything okay? Where are you? Did you find Xander?"

"Everything's fine," Oz replied. "I'm with Justine. Xander went home."

"Oh, well, I guess that's good." Willow shrugged, upset because Xander was obviously still mad at them for doubting his psychic power. "I mean, that's better than finding him dead in a ditch somewhere or something. Are you coming back to the Bronze?"

"No, I'll see you tomorrow." Oz paused. "As long as I'm here, I thought I'd have Justine do a Tarot reading for me, too. Can't hurt."

"No, I guess not." Willow handed the phone back to the bartender after Oz hung up, and hurried back to Buffy.

"What's the word?" Buffy asked.

"Xander's home and everything's fine." Willow smiled, but her nerves were still on edge and she couldn't quite figure out why.

Except . . . Justine is pretty free with her Tarot readings. . . .

CHAPTER 7

Friday after school, Buffy headed for downtown Sunnydale after checking in with Giles. He hadn't heard from Angel and no mystical calamities seemed to be brewing. *Just as well,* she thought. Among her friends, weirdness abounded.

Xander had skipped classes and he wasn't answering his phone. Oz hadn't been around, either. Willow hadn't even heard from him since the phone call at the Bronze last night. Willow had left during her free periods to work at the gallery. The art show seemed like the best place to find everyone, especially Xander.

Buffy was ready to swear Xander was an alien from another planet if that's what he wanted to believe. *Whatever it takes to get him out of this major mad.* She couldn't take another day of silent treatment, not from Xander-the-never-shuts-up. Until he had stopped talking, she hadn't realized how much she relied on his daily dose of quirk to keep her going. No matter how bad things got, Xander was always there to make her smile. *At least he tries.*

Willow looked up sharply when Buffy walked into the gallery. Her hopeful look changed to disappointment.

"What?" Buffy asked. "You're giving me a Cordelia look. Like I've got terminal color clash."

Willow shook her head. "I thought you might be Oz."

"Oh." Buffy dropped into the chair beside Willow. She lowered her voice so the volunteers breezing in and out wouldn't overhear. "You haven't heard from him yet?"

"I called a while ago, but no one answered. I bet the band jammed all night because Devon's back from L.A. You know, learning new songs, trying things out. He's probably still asleep."

"Could be." Buffy smiled, but she knew Willow didn't feel as casual as she sounded. "Something's bothering you, though. What?"

"Nothing." A shadow of doubt clouded Willow's pixie face. "Just the Tarot reading thing."

"What about it?" Buffy frowned.

Willow's brow furrowed. "Not that I really think Tarot can tell the future, but it's just that . . ." Willow sighed. "What if Justine sees something really bad in Oz's cards? With the wolf or something."

"Justine couldn't tell he was a werewolf from a Tarot reading, could she?" Buffy asked.

"That's probably not the usual interpretation of 'the beast within,' no." Willow grinned and slipped a floppy disk into the computer.

"Any sign of Xander?"

Willow shook her head. "No, but then that kind of fits in with the suddenly-not-speaking-to-anyone persona."

"Which is starting to wear on my nerves, believe it or not. I think I better go look for him."

Buffy headed straight for Justine's display through the light crowd browsing the art show. Over the weekend the sidewalks would be clogged with curious customers anxious to buy. At least Buffy hoped so. Her mother had been too frantic to say much more than good-bye on her way out the door that morning. She was working her heart out to make the Sunnydale Sidewalk Art Festival a huge success.

For the moment, the lack of activity worked in Buffy's favor as she searched for Xander. After a couple walked by Justine's display with only a passing glance, the artist planted her hands on her hips and shook her head. Clearly disgusted, she sat in a canvas chair beside a small table.

Obviously not on the fast track to artistic fame and fortune. As Buffy drew closer to the three-sided display, she could see why. Although Justine's imaginative pictures of winged horses, wizards, dragons, and other fantasy fare were beautifully executed, most people probably wouldn't want them hanging over their sofas. *Including me.*

Xander wasn't anywhere near Justine's display, but on a hunch, Buffy decided it couldn't hurt to take a Slayer reading on the artist. "Hi, Justine."

Justine hesitated. "You're . . . Xander's friend?"

"Buffy Summers. My mom is running the festival."

"Oh, yes." Justine nodded and perked up when Buffy leaned forward to study a painting of a black unicorn silhouetted against a full moon. "Interested?"

"Uh—no," Buffy said, noting the price tag. Her petty cash was a few hundred dollars short and the price of holy water had just gone up. "I've got a wall space deficit in my room."

Justine immediately lost interest.

"Has Xander been by today? Or Oz?" Buffy added as an afterthought.

"No." Justine shook her head, but the question obviously unsettled her. She nervously slipped her hand into her bulging pocket.

Checking to make sure she hasn't lost her wallet? Buffy wondered. *Or touching a lucky rabbit's foot?*

"Is that yours?" Spotting a Tarot card lying on the pavement, Buffy stooped over to pick it up.

"Don't!" Justine suddenly sprang forward, shoving Buffy aside.

Surprised, Buffy almost struck back, but caught herself. The artist was no match for a Slayer punch. Besides, she wouldn't learn anything if Justine was out cold.

"Don't *ever* touch my Tarot deck. *Ever!*" Justine's eyes narrowed and her voice seethed with rage as she picked up the card.

"I'm sorry, Justine." Genuinely perplexed, Buffy adopted an apologetic attitude. "I just saw it lying there and—"

"Forget it." Justine inserted the card into a Tarot deck she had pulled from her pocket. Instead of putting the deck back into her pocket, she held it tightly between both palms.

"Do you do readings professionally?" Buffy asked.

"No." Still gripping the cards, Justine stared at Buffy. "Is there something else?"

"Guess not." Buffy smiled and moved on with her instincts on full alert.

She hoped Giles was still at the library.

Giles looked up with a start when Buffy and Willow burst into his office. "What's happened?"

"Nothing. Something?" Buffy threw up her hands. "I don't know. That's why we came to you. To find out."

"I see." Giles kept a stack of Tarot reference books from toppling when Willow reached for the phone.

"Sorry." Willow dialed, then paced the length of the phone cord, which reached outside the office door. "Come on, Oz."

"Find out what exactly?" Giles frowned at Buffy, once again reminded that he wasn't privy to every little nuance of their lives.

"Hey! Are you okay, Oz?" Willow stepped outside the office pulling the phone cord taut.

"Oz has been low profile today," Buffy explained. "And Xander isn't talking."

Giles looked mildly surprised. "Meaning he's not forthcoming with information?"

Buffy shook her head. "Practically mute."

"That's rather a refreshing thought, actually." Giles cleared his throat. "Perhaps he's simply embarrassed because he realized he's not psychic."

"We thought of that," Willow said as she came back in. She replaced the receiver and sat down. "Oz is fine. Just sleepy. He stayed up all night working on some new songs Devon wants to add to the play list."

Buffy eyed Giles intently. "Why would Justine fly into a rage because I almost touched one of her Tarot cards?"

"A rage?" Giles shrugged when Buffy nodded. "I'd say that's an overreaction to the accepted principles of Tarot, but not without grounds."

"What principles?" Buffy asked.

Giles picked up his tea and leaned back. "The owner of a Tarot deck spends an inordinate amount of time handling the cards so they'll absorb the owner's specific psychic energies."

"Which explains why she carries her deck in her pocket." Buffy folded her arms, her thoughtful gaze on the floor.

"Yes, quite so," Giles agreed. "With the exception

of someone having a Tarot reading done, a foreign touch could contaminate the deck."

"So Oz and Xander had to touch the cards for their readings." Willow looked to Giles for clarification. "Like a personalized imprint?"

"Yes." Giles's gaze shot to Willow. "Oz had a Tarot reading from the same woman?"

"Justine," Willow said.

"Last night." Scowling slightly, Buffy began to pace.

"Kind of strange, huh?"

"I'm not sure I follow, Willow." Giles was aware that his young associates read evil portent into anything unusual no matter how minuscule. It had also been proven on several occasions that their instincts were usually correct. However, he failed to perceive a threat in the benign concept of Tarot.

"Well, it's just that Xander suddenly turns into Mr. Strong, Silent Type after he has a Tarot reading done . . . and prolonged seclusion isn't his usual M.O."

"Meaning he went home rather than meeting us at the Bronze last night," Buffy added in response to Giles's puzzled look.

"And you suspect some sort of supernatural foul play may be responsible?" Giles asked. "As opposed to the possibility that Xander simply may have been too tired or depressed to join you."

"Or maybe he just isn't ready to talk about the psychic thing." Willow shrugged. "Especially after he made such a big deal about it."

"Possibly, but this is Hellmouth country." Buffy unfolded her arms and straightened. "What if Justine is some kind of demonic femme fatale that attracts unsuspecting men for some unknown evil purpose? Xander wouldn't be able to resist the bait."

Willow looked up sharply. "Oz is usually a bait-resistant guy."

"Of course he is," Buffy said quickly. "Unless Justine's secret weapon isn't just a pretty face."

Although wary of jumping to conclusions, Giles wasn't willing to dismiss Buffy's concerns out of hand. "It might be prudent to investigate just to be sure."

Buffy's eyes lit up. "I was hoping you'd say that."

"Did you bring your stake?" Willow glanced toward the sun as it vanished behind the low Sunnydale skyline.

Buffy patted her back pocket and scanned the Golden Lantern parking lot for Justine's green van. "The dragon-mobile isn't here, but the art show just closed down. Justine could get back any minute."

"We don't need her crashing the snoop party." Willow's joking tone masked her uneasiness. They had reached Xander's mom by phone before they left Giles's apartment. Buffy had convinced Mrs. Harris to check and Xander was asleep on his basement sofa. *Probably zonked from sitting in the sun with Justine all day.* Still, it was odd that both Xander and Oz had developed acute fatigue.

And Justine's Tarot readings are the only thing they have in common lately, Willow thought as she jogged across the pavement behind the Slayer. If Justine *was* a mystic meanie, they had to find out without losing the stealth advantage.

"Which room?" Willow whispered. Most of the windows in the long, one-story building were dark.

Buffy shrugged as she walked to the first lighted window. The curtains were drawn, but as in most cheap motels, they were too small for the window and didn't meet in the middle. She peeked inside and jumped back. "Short, bald man in bathroom. No way he's Justine in disguise."

"Probably not." Willow wrinkled her nose. The next lighted room was empty except for an open suitcase. She began to lose hope of turning up anything that would prove or disprove the Justine-is-evil theory, but they hit the jackpot in the last unit on the end.

"This is her." Buffy pointed through the partially open curtain. "I saw her work today and those paintings are shining examples of her freaky period."

Willow edged closer to Buffy. Unless they were locked in the bathroom, there was no sign of Xander or Oz. The four large canvases on the bed and leaning against the wall looked like Tarot card images. Nothing else about the room looked strange.

"Those must be the pieces Justine wanted to finish," Buffy said. "Guess she didn't have time."

"Guess not," Willow said, her gaze drawn back to the paintings. The first two, a winged angel and a dark tower, had not progressed past the black and gray contrasts of the underlying pencil sketches. Some light color washes had been applied to the painting with the devil figure. The colors in the Grim Reaper-stalks-bleak-desert picture were more vibrant, but the details were still vague.

"Uh-oh." Buffy grabbed Willow's arm and pulled her around the corner of the building.

"What?" Willow whispered from the safety of the shadows, then shrank back when she saw the green van. "Do you think she saw us?"

"No, but—" Buffy tensed. She palmed her stake as Justine pulled the van into the parking space in front of the room. Several yards away, a dark figure eased out of the overgrown shrubbery that separated the unlit parking lot from the alley behind the neighboring mini-mall.

"Vampire?" Willow whispered as the figure crept toward Justine's van.

Buffy nodded. "I'll dust. You distract Justine."

"Okay." Willow took a deep breath and stepped into the weak light cast by fixtures attached to the building. "Hey, Justine!"

The artist looked up from the far side of the van and slammed the door closed. She smiled as she approached the room door. "Hi, there. What's up?"

From the corner of her eye, Willow saw the vampire suddenly change direction to run away from the motel. Buffy whirled to give chase. She moved closer to Justine and blurted the first excuse she could think of for skulking around the woman's motel. "Uh—have you seen Oz?"

"Not since I did a Tarot reading for him last night." Justine peered into the dark when scuffling, rattling sounds behind the neighboring mini-mall rose above the white noise of passing traffic. "What's that?"

"Cats!" Willow said louder than she intended. "Getting into the trash." She quickly changed the subject. "Xander said you did a reading for him, too. I've dabbled with it myself a little."

"Really?" Justine turned to unlock the door.

"But I've never had a reading done," Willow added. "Not a real one with an ... expert. But I've always wanted to, you know, get a glimpse of my future."

"I'd be happy to do one for you." Justine pulled her Tarot deck from her pocket and held it out. "If you've got time. I don't charge anything like those phony TV people."

"Oh, well ... uh ..." Willow hesitated, wondering why Justine seemed so eager. Did she just believe in the soul-searching aspects of Tarot and her abilities? *Or is there some creepy agenda?*

Willow heard the faint *whack* of the Slayer's stake striking undead flesh followed by the *whoosh* of vanishing vampire.

But since Buffy's here as backup, Willow thought, *now might be a good time to find out.*

She reached out to touch the deck.

Justine yanked it back when Buffy suddenly appeared out of the dark. "Buffy! You startled me. What are you doing here?"

"Just hanging out on a Friday night." Buffy glanced at the cards in Justine's hand.

Afraid Buffy might counter her cover story, Willow jumped in. "Oz isn't here, but Justine said she'd do a Tarot reading for me. Free even."

Buffy nodded. "Sounds like fun. Can I watch?"

"Not a good idea." Justine faltered under Buffy's curious scrutiny and quickly explained her remark. "It's just that a Tarot reading is a very personal thing . . . for the subject."

Willow realized that Buffy was baiting the artist, pushing for a reaction. "Well, then maybe Buffy can have a reading done, too!"

"Great idea." Buffy smiled, but her eyes were hard on the artist. "Forewarned is forearmed, right?"

"What does that mean?" Justine snapped.

Buffy held the woman's narrowed gaze. "More than I meant it to, apparently."

When Justine bristled, Willow intervened to diffuse the tension. "I think Buffy just meant that if you know what's in the future and you don't like it, you can change it. Right, Justine?"

Justine nodded. "Yes. Free will is always a factor."

"Right, so let's get started," Willow said with feigned enthusiasm.

"Actually, I'm a little tired. How about we do it some other time." Justine opened her door and darted inside.

Willow raised an eyebrow when they heard the security chain slip into place beyond the closed door. "So should I be worried now?" she asked Buffy.

"I'm hovering between concerned and anxious."

Justine pulled the curtain closed, then settled on the bed. Setting the Tarot deck on the nightstand, she hugged a pillow to her chest. The unexpected visit from Oz and Xander's friends was disturbing. She had made Oz leave a message with Willow's parents and then sent him home after the Tarot reading with instructions to stay put. However, she couldn't monitor Oz's every move in the beginning phases of the transition. Something must have happened to make Willow come looking for him.

Justine picked up the phone and dialed the number Oz had given her. He answered after four rings. She hung up without speaking.

If Willow and Buffy were really looking for Oz, they would have called or gone to his house, Justine thought uneasily. *Oz is home, so that isn't why they were checking out my room.*

Troubled, Justine retrieved her deck. She had to know if the two girls represented a new, unforeseen obstacle between her and her goal.

Justine held the cards between her palms, her eyes closed in calming meditation for a moment before she shuffled. She decided to use a straight, five card spread rather than the Celtic cross pattern she had dealt for Xander and Oz's readings.

Sitting cross-legged on the bed, Justine dealt the first card. The Eight of Pentacles, a coin craftsman, represented all the hard work she had put into the project. This was no less than she expected.

The second card, the Six of Wands, depicting a victorious horseman carrying a wand, assured her that she had successfully completed the necessary tasks so far. No surprise there, either.

She paused and took a deep breath. If something had dramatically changed her prospects for the future, it would be revealed in the third, pivotal card in the spread.

Justine turned over the Queen of Wands and inhaled sharply. A new element she had not seen in previous readings had been added to the equation.

Whether or not she achieved her ultimate goal depended on a blond woman with blue-green eyes.

Not Willow, then. Buffy.

Needing more information, Justine decided to deal an extra card. She flipped the fourth card on top of the third instead of using it in the five-card pattern and gasped.

The Magician, one of the twenty-two Major Arcana cards. Its meaning was unmistakable. The woman represented by the Queen of Wands was extremely powerful, with the ability to cast those energies against her.

Justine stared at the pivotal pair of cards, as certain as she could be without positive proof that Buffy was the key to her success or failure.

There's only one way to find out, Justine thought.

The next two cards, the fifth and sixth now because of the additional card, were indicators of the probable future. She turned over the Wheel Of Fortune—upside-down. The meaning of the ancient Tarot symbol was not as easy to interpret as the first three. Did it represent a complete reversal of fortune or that she was destined to reap what she had sown?

Stumped, Justine dealt the last card.

The Tower.

Conflict and the destruction of my current way of life, she thought. *In essence, exactly what I hope to achieve.*

Justine leaned back. An obstacle had been put in her path, but that did not necessarily mean all was lost. The probable futures portrayed by the cards were not absolute. She had free will. Taking action could alter the shifting course of fate indicated in the new reading.

Smiling, Justine turned toward the unfinished painting of Judgment—the battle between good and evil.

And the only weapon she needed to defeat the Queen of Wands.

CHAPTER 8

"**W**hat's this?" Giles held the paper bag spotted with grease at arm's length.

"Hamburgers, fries, and chocolate shakes." Buffy set the cardboard drink container on the study table. "I can't brainstorm on an empty stomach." Giles and Willow joined her at the table.

"What did you find out on your expedition?" Giles asked.

"Not much," Buffy said, "but there's definitely something up with Justine."

"She's protected." Angel entered the library so quietly Buffy hadn't even sensed him. Her heart leaped into her throat at the sight of him.

"By whom?" Giles asked.

"Or what?" Willow unwrapped a burger and dumped a few fries on the paper.

"I don't know, but something's been making Willy's customers nervous enough to lie low." Angel moved around the table to stand by the stairs, joining them while maintaining a discreet distance. "It's emanating from Justine."

"How do you know?" Buffy sipped her shake.

Angel glanced at Buffy from under hooded eyes. "I felt it when I followed you to her motel."

"Playing guardian Angel again, huh?" Buffy teased, but she was elated.

"Felt what exactly, Angel?" Giles winced slightly as Willow bit into her burger.

"Repelled," Angel answered simply.

"Intriguing." Giles shifted his glance to Buffy and back to Willow. "Did either of you sense anything threatening from this woman?"

"No, not threatening," Willow said. "First Justine wanted to do a Tarot reading for me and since I knew Buffy was there, it seemed like a good idea because it might have given us a clue. I mean, in case anything weird happened, which it didn't. But Justine changed her mind after Buffy showed up."

Buffy nodded. "She protects that Tarot deck like her life depends on it."

"Which is not unusual as we discussed earlier." Giles pulled a shake from the cardboard holder. "Anything else?"

Buffy looked at him askance as he shoved a straw into the shake. "Just the Tarot paintings."

"*Big* Tarot paintings," Willow added. "In various stages of being finished."

"I see." Giles paused thoughtfully and took a sip. "Paintings of what cards?"

"The dead guy wearing the hooded cloak looked like it was almost done." Buffy tore open another packet of ketchup.

"That would be Death," Giles said.

Angel leaned against the banister. Buffy sensed his discomfort. *Because of Justine or just his garden-variety tortured soul issues?*

Willow swallowed. "Then there was the devil with some chained people, a winged angel surrounded by fire and a dark tower in a storm."

"The Devil, Judgment, and the Tower. Interesting." Giles reached for one of Buffy's fries.

Buffy playfully slapped his hand away and handed him his own packet. "What happened to American food—bad?"

"I'm hungry." Giles adjusted his glasses and folded his hands. "All four are Major Arcana cards, from the original Tarot before the suit cards were added."

"What do they mean?" Willow asked.

"Whether for good or bad depends on how the cards are dealt, but each of these four represents a specific aspect of change." Giles picked up a fry and nibbled the end.

"Such as?" Buffy prompted.

"Death deals with the past and the future," Giles explained. "The Devil in matters of life decisions that seem too confining. The Tower represents rapid change arising from destruction. Judgment, however, is a bit more complex."

"How so?" Willow wiped her chin with a napkin.

Giles ate another fry before going on. "Judgment could mean anything from breaking free of seemingly helpless circumstances—"

Too close to home for comfort, Buffy thought with a guarded glance at Angel. Their relationship—or lack thereof—was one of the most helpless circumstances she'd known.

"—or simply being accountable for one's actions. It also represents the universal conflict between good and evil."

"And all this could be a threat because?" Buffy forced her attention back to matters at hand and looked at Giles levelly.

"I'm not sure there is a threat," Giles admitted. "Tarot is harmless except when the uneducated take their readings too literally and act foolishly as a result."

"Like Xander." Willow sighed.

"We don't know what Justine told Oz," Buffy pointed out. "Maybe we should ask."

Willow winced. "I'm not sure I want to know. What if it's something wolf-related? That excludes me?"

"I can't see that happening, but I'll ask for you if you'd like." Buffy didn't press Willow, although it wasn't hard to figure out she was worried about how she fit into Oz's future. A cosmic crowbar couldn't pry them apart, but only time would prove it. "Be right back."

Buffy slipped into the office and closed the door to use the phone. After several rings Oz answered. "Hey, Oz. Catch up on your sleep?"

"Yes."

Silence.

"Listen, I'm at the library with Willow. She's a little concerned . . . about the Tarot reading you had last night. I know it's silly and she shouldn't be, but something about Justine seems off. What happened? With the reading, I mean."

"Nothing."

"Oh, well, that's good, I guess. I just thought I'd ask. I guess we were overreacting." Buffy waited, but Oz didn't respond. "Oz, if possible, you're even more stoic than usual," she stated flatly.

"I'm fine." Oz hung up.

Buffy exhaled as she replaced the receiver. Something was definitely wrong, but it didn't have anything to do with Oz's feelings toward Willow. Oz tended to be verbally economical, but never abrupt.

"What did he say?" Willow asked when Buffy returned to the study table.

"Yes, nothing, and I'm fine," Buffy said. "In that order."

"That's rather terse even for Oz. This increases the likelihood that Justine's reading has cast some sort of hold over him and Xander." Giles shoved a half-eaten hamburger aside.

His disgust apparently winning out over his appetite, Buffy thought with amusement.

Willow stood up. "I need to go see him."

"No, Willow." Buffy gently pushed her back down. "You've got a long night of heavy duty research ahead. That's the best way I can think of for you to help Oz."

"Using my head." Willow nodded. "Okay."

Buffy glanced toward Giles. "This whole Tarot thing reeks of bad, Giles. What else do you know about it?"

"Not a lot, actually." Giles motioned toward the stack of books on the far end of the table. "I've been reading, though. It's widely believed that Tarot was introduced into Europe by Gypsies in the fourteenth century."

Angel looked up. He had his own personal history with gypsies.

"Gypsies?" Buffy stared, an acquired reaction to the power of the Romani who had restored Angel's soul. "So we could be dealing with a curse."

"Perhaps." Giles frowned. "The Gypsies began to migrate to Europe in the late thirteen hundreds from Hindustan, where they worshiped the dark goddess, Kali."

"Kali." Willow shuddered. "She's bad, right?"

"Very," Giles agreed. "As legend has it, Kali was charged with maintaining cosmic order. She will ultimately achieve perfect order when the universe ends."

"So we might be facing a demonic plot to end the *universe?*" Buffy's eyes widened. "The *whole* universe as in everything?"

"Sounds like Kali's more ambitious than your average demon," Willow mumbled.

"Let's not jump to conclusions," Giles cautioned. "A connection between Justine, Tarot, and Kali seems like a stretch, but further investigation is probably warranted."

"A background check on Justine wouldn't hurt, either." Willow moved to the chair in front of the computer.

"And while you're covering the research, Angel and I will go get Xander and Oz," Buffy said. Angel was already headed toward the door. She followed him, suddenly remembering that she was also supposed to be keeping Sunnydale safe for her mom's imported artists. The blood-starved crypt set had been awake and possibly prowling since the sun had set hours ago.

The streets were not quiet. It was after ten on a Friday night and groups of students and work-weary adults were unwinding in restaurants and clubs. Although the art show was closed until the morning, many of the artists had lingered to talk with new friends after packing up their wares. The absence of widespread panic was reassuring, though.

"Just how powerful is Justine's vampire repellant?" Buffy asked Angel when they reached Oz's house. They hadn't encountered anyone of demonic heritage on the trip from the library.

"Not enough to stop them from feeding." Angel paused to scan the darkened house. "Oz isn't here."

Buffy forced her mind from the thought of Angel's acute ability to detect the scent of warm blood. No lights and no van in the driveway were another dead giveaway. "I call Oz, Oz leaves. Why?"

Angel shook his head. "Maybe there's no connection."

"Maybe." Buffy fretted as she retreated to the sidewalk. She had no idea where Oz had gone and little hope of finding him unless he showed up at one of their regular spots. *Giles's place? The Bronze? Xander's?*—

"Xander." Buffy charged back down the street.

Willow huddled over the computer. She had finally managed to hack into the records of another California sidewalk art show that had been held in Lancaster, seventy-five miles north of L.A. two weeks ago.

"Justine participated in this one, too." Willow closed out of the site and started a search for the local newspaper.

Giles sat back, chewing on the end of his glasses. "That makes six in the past two months."

Willow nodded, trying not to let her mounting panic interfere with the research. In each of the previous five towns where Justine's presence at an art show had been confirmed, three people had lapsed into mysterious comas and died. "I'm checking the news archives in the local paper. Hang on a sec."

"This is all nonsense." Giles set a fifteenth-century expose regarding the superstitious practices of Romani tribes aside. "Hysteria over imagined heresy."

"This is so not good." Willow looked up from the monitor. "Three comatose people have since died in and around Lancaster, too. No medical reason found."

"Eighteen in all." Giles rubbed his chin. "Definitely a pattern, but to what purpose?"

Willow shook her head and glanced at her watch, wishing Buffy would get back. *Preferably with Oz and Xander in tow.* She didn't want to jump to conclusions, but deadly trends never turned out to be mere coincidences when they hit Sunnydale.

Giles stood up, distracting her from her worst case scenario thoughts. "I'm going to look for another volume." He disappeared back in the stacks.

As Willow started another Internet search, she heard something outside the double doors.

"Willow!" Oz called.

Oz! Willow charged out the doors and stopped. She checked an impulse to throw her arms around her dazed and rumpled boyfriend. "What's going on, Oz?"

"Come on." Oz waved her to follow as he turned. "Xander's in trouble."

"Where? What trouble? Buffy went to find you— both of you—but . . ."

Oz didn't look back as he rushed down the main corridor toward the front entrance. Willow followed him outside and paused as he kept going toward the van parked on the street.

"Wait!" Willow hesitated. Something about Oz's movement wasn't right, like he had short-circuited his internal wiring. Still, she couldn't just stand there and let him leave. *What if he disappears* again?

Willow stepped back into the library and yelled. Her voice reverberated through the empty halls. "Giles! I'm going with Oz to help Xander! I'll call!"

Willow dashed across the campus toward the van. Oz pulled away from the curb a split second after she piled into the passenger seat. "So—we're off to rescue Xander, right?"

Staring straight ahead, Oz nodded and drove.

Unnerved by his silence, Willow watched the pavement and the traffic whiz by. Something had obviously muffled Oz, but maybe he was taking action because he couldn't talk! She really wanted to believe Oz was still capable of resistance. *If not, maybe I'm being kidnapped by my boyfriend.*

Giles heard Willow call as he exited the stacks and headed for the doors. "Help Xander? I thought Buffy—"

Disturbed by Willow's hasty departure, Giles stared down the empty corridor. *Why would Willow run off with Oz when they suspected Oz was under some manner of evil influence?* The question nagged until he realized that she wouldn't. Moreover, it was difficult to imagine that even-tempered, loyal Oz's intentions were less than aboveboard.

Giles returned to the library and settled in at the study table to address the implications of unexplained comas and Justine's art shows. He picked up the Tarot deck he had been using for reference and separated the cards into five piles: one for each of the four suits, Wands, Pentacles, Cups, and Swords; and the fifth for the twenty-two cards of the Major Arcana.

Giles set the suit piles aside and spread the Major Arcana cards across the table. Then, with pen in hand and a notebook at the ready, he studied the more powerful cards in the original Gypsy Tarot deck. After several moments, he separated out the four images Willow had described in Justine's unfinished paintings. Nothing clicked.

He doodled in the notebook, letting his mind drift from one tidbit of information to another: eighteen people dead, six towns, four paintings, Justine. He shuffled through the suit cards: four suits, fourteen cards in each for a total of fifty-six. Twenty-two cards in the Major Arcana.

Four paintings plus eighteen deaths equals twenty-two.

He wrote down the equation and circled it as a theory began to form. His train of thought was derailed when the library doors blasted open.

"Walk!" Buffy ordered.

"What's this?" Giles frowned as Xander shuffled in. He moved slowly and stiffly, as though every awkward step was a monumental effort.

"Xander the living zombie, apparently. He was like this when Angel and I found him." Taking Xander's arm, she steered him to a chair. "Sit."

Xander sat.

"At least he obeys voice commands." Buffy exhaled as Giles stepped up beside her. "Without the wonders of verbal remote control I never would have gotten him over here."

Giles waved his hand in front of Xander's staring eyes. Not even a blink.

By the time Oz turned into the Golden Lantern parking lot, Willow knew he was fighting a desperate internal battle. He gripped the steering wheel so hard his knuckles turned white and his skin was damp with sweat.

I just can't tell if he's winning or losing, Willow thought fretfully. *Bringing me to Justine's motel certainly isn't a good sign—except that she's not here.*

No light shone from the motel room and the artist's green dragon-mobile was gone. Willow breathed a little easier.

So where did Justine go this late? Willow wondered as she slipped out of the van and warily followed Oz. *Is Xander with her? Or locked in the bathroom or*—Willow froze when Justine appeared in the darkened doorway.

"Hello, Willow." Justine smiled. "Come on in."

"Uh—no, that's okay. We were just passing by and . . . thought you might want to go *out!* For coffee or—" Willow lurched, thrown off balance when Oz grabbed her arm and dragged her by Justine. She was too stunned by the betrayal to struggle.

Justine closed the door, secured the chain, and flipped on a light. The room had been stripped of everything except the unfinished Tower painting.

"Have a seat." Justine patted the bed.

Oz perched on the edge of the mattress.

Willow stared into Oz's glazed eyes, her heart breaking. "What happened to you?"

"He can't answer," Justine said. "Not unless I tell him to. His free will—what's left of it—has been totally subverted to mine."

"What does that mean?" Willow knew she was trapped. But contrary to Justine's obvious beliefs, she wasn't completely helpless, either. The tide of many battles often turned on information.

And delay, she thought, sitting down so Justine wouldn't feel threatened. Her only shot was to keep Justine talking. *Until Buffy shows up—hopefully before I lose my mind, too.*

"Oz's emotional and mental essence is being transferred into my Devil card painting. Death has almost finished absorbing Xander's." Justine answered with an air of arrogance, obviously confident that nothing could stop or hurt her.

Willow clenched her jaw, trying not to let her revulsion and fear show. "Is that why those two paintings looked more finished?"

"Yes." Justine glanced to the single canvas left in the room. "You're perfect for the Tower."

Willow didn't react openly, but her mind reeled. Giles had said the Tower represented rapid change—based on destruction. *How does that fit me?*

"That's not possible," Willow stated defiantly.

Justine took the bait. "It is if one has tapped into the power of Kali—the supreme goddess of chaos."

CHAPTER 9

Buffy curbed her impatience while Giles mulled over Xander's transformation into Robot Man. She knew exactly how her Watcher felt. It had taken her a few minutes to adjust when she and Angel had found Xander stretched out in his basement. Totally spaced pretty much described his condition.

"Apparently, Oz isn't experiencing the same symptoms." Giles shook Xander's shoulder, but there was no response. The boy just sat there.

"Beats me. I haven't seen Oz. Angel's still out looking for him."

"He came here to get Willow." Giles snapped his head around. "To help Xander."

"And Willow went with him? When?" Buffy instantly shifted gears. If Oz was following the same pattern of mindless decline as Xander, she had to move quickly.

"Half an hour ago give or take a few minutes." A trace of panic flicked across Giles's face. "It's imperative that you intercept Willow before she encounters Justine."

"That's not just a hunch, is it?"

"No." Giles followed Buffy to the library doors. "Eighteen people have died in the wake of Justine's art show schedule over the past two months. If my suspicions are correct, Xander and Oz are slipping into fatal comas Justine induced with her Tarot readings."

"Why?" Buffy paused.

"I have no idea—yet."

"Kali? What's that got to do with Tarot?" Perched on the bed beside Oz, Willow faked a puzzled look, as though she had never heard of the Hindu goddess.

"Do you really want to know?" Justine asked smugly.

"Yeah, I do, because—well, the idea of a magickal deck of cards is a little ridiculous. A lot ridiculous, actually." Willow felt a tinge of triumph when Justine stiffened. Turning the artist's own über-confidence against her might buy her time and information. *Although, anything I learn won't be worth much if Buffy doesn't get here soon,* Willow thought. *Before my brain is scrambled.*

Justine glared for a moment, then smiled. "Why

not? It's an interesting tale. But be forewarned, this isn't a story with a happy ending."

Willow didn't react, but she was very aware of Oz sitting beside her. The merry spark that always lit up his eyes was gone, and except for breathing, he hadn't moved. *But he's alive, so he's not lost, yet.*

Justine pulled the Tarot deck from her pocket. "This deck was created by Hovan Ramos, a Gypsy and one of my ancestors. I found it hidden in my grandmother's cellar, locked in a box with a journal he wrote six hundred years ago."

"Wow," Willow muttered, more impressed than her tone suggested. Justine didn't seem to notice.

"Hovan was a Romani magician." Justine played with the cards, fanning the deck, then shuffling, which Willow knew was supposed to infuse the Tarot with a constant stream of her psychic energy. "His dream was to end the persecution the Gypsy tribes suffered throughout Europe, to create a world where the Romani were the most powerful and respected people."

"Those wacky Gypsies . . ." Willow trailed off.

"Yes, they were ambitious." Justine went on. "Tarot is the Romani link to the human heart, mind, and soul; our window to all time in the universe—past, present, and future. Hovan chose it as the tool to remake the world. He made this deck, coloring each card with painstaking precision, and when it was finished, he called on Kali for help."

Willow shifted nervously. The Romani were extraordinarily gifted in the magickal arts. *And apparently they've got connections in high underworld places, too.* She did not doubt a word of Justine's story.

The artist's dark eyes burned with fervor as she continued. "Kali appeared to him suspended between this world and the nether world. Her essence, however, was not barred. She empowered the deck with a wisp of her existence, preserving it against the ravages of time."

Willow detected a slight frown when Justine paused. *A sign of insecurity? Hard to tell,* she mused, *but any weakness is a plus for us . . . if we know what it is.*

"What went wrong?" Willow asked. "Something did because the Romani don't rule the world."

"Nothing went wrong," Justine snapped. "Hovan never imprinted the deck with his psychic energy. He never used it."

"Why not?"

"Irrelevant." Justine smiled. "It's mine now, along with Hovan's journal, which gave me the keys to the deck's power. Anyone who touches it is immediately under my control."

Tell me something I didn't guess, Willow thought with a worried glance at Oz.

"And of course, once you've touched the deck, I can do a reading, which begins the transfer of your essence into the chosen card. After all twenty-two Major Arcana paintings are empowered, I'll have the ultimate Tarot."

"Meaning?" Willow slipped her hands underneath her.

"Normally, Tarot foretells what *might* be. The new deck of Major Arcana cards will create what *will* be." Justine leaned against the dresser and glanced at the charmed cards.

"Well, uh—what if it doesn't create what you want?"

"It will." Justine caught Willow's skeptical look and quickly explained. "Because I control the deal, I can mold the world by manipulating the fates of important people. And they don't even have to be present!"

"So you'll be what?" Willow asked. "Rich? Famous? Queen of the Gypsies?"

"Whatever I want, starting with a one-woman show at the most prestigious gallery in New York." Justine huffed, disgusted. "Hovan was a fool not to take advantage of the opportunity."

The implications were staggering, but Willow had met enough demons and their power-struck accomplices to know they never did something for nothing. *And usually the price is too high. A bad news detail Justine hasn't considered . . . or doesn't want to.*

"Unless he had second thoughts," Willow said. "What does Kali want?"

"Perfect order on Earth—as quickly as possible." Justine shrugged. "Not a big deal."

"Very big deal." Willow tensed, remembering something Giles had said. "There can't be perfect order until the universe ends because, well . . . *nothing* is as orderly as anything can get."

She didn't mention that a New York gallery show was a paltry prize in exchange for universal order.

"Spare me." Justine rolled her eyes and stood. "I've got a Tarot deck to finish."

"No, thanks." Willow lunged for the door holding out hope she would escape or find Buffy racing to save her.

"Get her!" Justine barked.

Oz leaped off the bed and grabbed Willow around the waist as she fumbled with the chain.

This isn't Oz, Willow told herself, *just his empty, hijacked body.* She kicked and clawed at the vicelike arms, but couldn't stop Oz from dragging her back to the bed. *Okay, he's stronger, but I'm smarter—right now, anyway.* Willow screamed.

"Shut up! Shut her up!"

Oz sprawled across Willow and clamped a hand over her mouth.

With Oz's weight pressing on her chest and his hand blocking her mouth and nose, Willow couldn't breathe. She stopped struggling, but she didn't give up. She couldn't escape the controlling power of the Hovan Tarot deck, but maybe she could dampen the effects.

"Are you going to be quiet?" Justine asked.

Willow nodded and gulped air when Oz took his hand away. As Justine moved toward her with the deck, Willow closed her eyes and whispered, "As the river flows let the mind be open to the sea. As the river flows let the mind be open—"

Oz pried open Willow's clenched fist and Justine slipped the charmed Tarot deck into her hand.

From the hazy, but quickly-solidifying dungeon in the Devil painting, Oz was helpless to stop his actions against Willow.

He had found himself trapped in a bizarre dual reality when he had awakened that morning, simultaneously aware of his real surroundings and the world within the painting. His mind spanned the stream of consciousness that bridged his body and the painting, allowing him to perceive both realities even though the painting wasn't present in the motel room.

Willow's squeal was muffled as he clamped his hand over her mouth. Her large eyes widened in angry fear as she fought. He had always worried that his wolf-self might someday hurt Willow. He had never expected to turn his human hand against her.

His only consolation was the hope that Willow understood he had no choice. From the moment he had lured her out of the library, he had tried to break free of the heavy chains that bound him—and failed. Now, he retreated into the torment of the Devil card to escape the torment of the role he played in Willow's capture.

Enraged, Oz shrieked and struggled against the manacles and chains that bound him. Cold metal cut into his wrists and ankles. The pain focused his thoughts and he realized that his connection with reality was fading at an ever-quickening rate. He gazed beyond the horned demon perched on a high ledge toward the opening in the walls that enclosed him. Black moss grew in grotesque abandon from cracks in the damp stone. The stream of light pouring through the small window mocked him like the devil creature guarding it.

Like the wolf that consumed him three nights a month, there was no escape from the Devil's dungeon.

He had learned to cope with the wolf rather than letting it control his life. Now Justine had stolen his future, one that might have been bright. In spite of the artist's intent to rip off his mind with the Tarot reading, the truths and conclusions revealed by the cards had been incredibly accurate.

Oz remembered it all in detail. He replayed the reading in his mind to keep himself from going mad with grief.

His identity card had been the Knight of Wands. *"Black knight on an unknown quest,"* Justine had said.

Quest for what? Oz wondered again as he had last night. He didn't want anything more than to be with Willow and play music. He already had that.

Justine had drawn the Six of Swords as his second, covering card—success in spite of his anxieties. That had struck him oddly at the time. He wasn't anxious about anything more earthshaking than missing a chord during a paying gig.

Then the Devil card had shown. Discontent and an

inability to control his needs and desires—according to Justine. Oz had to discount the card's implication. He had adjusted to the werewolf. He could adjust to anything.

Except losing Willow.

Oz peered through the still fuzzy dungeon walls into the motel room and stared at the woman he wanted more than anything, including the musical success foretold by the Eight of Pentacles that represented his life's work.

Willow's expression became increasingly remote as Justine proceeded with the Tarot reading that would siphon her persona and will into the Tower painting.

There, Oz realized, Willow would be alone in the midst of a chaotic storm.

Anger and despair surged from deep inside him. Oz shook his imagined fists, but the chains and manacles continued to hold.

The Devil laughed.

Oz forced himself to calm down, but the rage was a reminder of the dual nature depicted by the Two of Pentacles. Justine couldn't possibly know about the wolf, which made that particular element of the reading all the more fascinating.

Having the moon card turn up had startled him, until Justine's interpretation put it into proper perspective regarding his artistic abilities. The one thing he was committed to besides Willow was music. Success was relative. As long as he could play and get by, he'd be happy.

Now he might not get the chance to achieve those modest goals.

A shiver ripped through Oz's psyche. Staying sane in the confines of his Tarot prison depended on his unshakable belief that Buffy and Giles would find a way to release him.

And Willow.

The hell Justine had created in her painting was nothing compared to the hell of knowing he had inadvertently betrayed the one person in the world he would gladly die to save.

CHAPTER 10

Buffy had no idea what time it was as she raced through Sunnydale toward the Golden Lantern Motel. Late, she realized as she turned onto the main avenue and crossed to the other side of the street. The artists' display booths, locked up or stripped of pictures and crafts, lined the deserted sidewalks like skeletal sentinels. All the stores were closed, although small groups of people still wandered in and out of clubs and restaurants. Buffy hoped everyone else was safely tucked in at home or hotel.

"Buffy!" Anya called above the screech of tires. She stopped her car in the middle of the street, cranked the wheel, and parked at a skewed angle a few feet away from the curb. Her scowl was dark enough to protect a vamp from the sun.

Annoyed, Buffy just wanted to get rid of the lovesick girl. So did Xander at last report, and she was pretty sure Giles wouldn't disapprove of a tiny fib that kept Anya at town's length. Anticipating the question, Buffy answered, "I haven't seen Xander . . . lately."

"He's probably at the Bronze with that artist." Anya shoved the gearshift into park when the car started to roll. "I'm looking for Willow."

Buffy was suddenly wary. "What do you want with Willow?"

"To help me cast a slow death by putting a rapid aging spell on Justine. Instant wrinkles and long life." Anya smiled and shifted again. "And she said *I'd* be sorry."

Buffy was off and running before Anya clipped a bumper steering away from the curb.

The motel was on the opposite side of Sunnydale from Giles's place. The closer she got, the more she feared she was too late. She never expected to barrel around a corner and see Oz and Willow walking toward her.

"Willow!" Buffy stopped, taking a deep breath of relief. "Where have you—" The words died in her throat as the catatonic couple simply parted to walk around her. "You're obviously not just out for a midnight stroll."

Buffy whirled, then sprang as the light changed. She jumped in front of Willow and Oz, her hands outstretched as they stepped off the curb into oncoming traffic. "Stop!"

A car whizzed by, horn blaring.

Recognizing the same automaton state as Xander's, Buffy yelled and pushed her friends to get them moving in reverse. "Back! Back!"

Willow and Oz stepped back onto the sidewalk and kept backing up.

"Halt!" Another wave of relief washed over Buffy when they obeyed. Their response time was better than Xander's, which would make navigating back to the library a lot easier. "At least I had a practice round with Xander," she muttered as she moved behind the pair.

"Buff—"

"Will?" Buffy turned the girl to face her. "Did you just talk?"

"Ho-van." Willow's intense struggle to speak didn't show in the void of her expression and eyes, but she squeezed the word out of a mouth clamped shut by tense muscle and rigid bone.

"Hovan," Buffy repeated. "What does that mean?"

"New." Willow swallowed. "Deck."

"Deck? Like in boat? Redwood?" Buffy paused. "Tarot! Which is so obvious."

"Cree . . . ate." Sweat coated Willow's brow. "F-fat."

"Create fat?" Buffy paused. "Or, okay, you probably mean 'fate'—unless Kali's got some twisted anti-weight-loss agenda," she hurried along, sensing that Willow was losing her limited vocal powers.

"Kah-li. Per-fect or . . . or-der."

"Got it. Kali's perfect order." Buffy turned Willow back around. She didn't want to tax her strength.

They had a long trek across town. The sooner Giles had Willow's clues the sooner he'd figure out what evil mojo Justine had used to turn her friends into remote-control dummies.

Seated at the table, Giles wrote down the words Willow had transmitted to Buffy. "Fate?"

"That's what she said. Well, actually, she said 'fat,' but considering the events of the past few days, I'm going to go with 'fate'." Buffy finished positioning Oz and Willow against the base of the upper book level and stood back. Giles had moved Xander to the floor, where he sat canted to the left against the stairs. "Sit!"

Willow and Oz sank into sitting positions on the floor without hesitation. The effect would have been comical if not for the seriousness of their condition and Justine's unknown scheme. Giles turned his attention back to the riddle.

Fate? He wrote the word again, then again. "Yes, I think that's the logical conclusion to draw."

"Maybe. Talking at all was a major effort." With the zombie brigade secured, Buffy sat down beside the librarian.

"Create fate." Giles stared at the words.

"There was one other thing," Buffy said. "Something about 'Kali's perfect order.' "

"Kali?" Giles grabbed his notes and doodles regarding the mysterious deaths that had occurred in towns Justine had visited across the state.

"So what's going on?" Buffy asked. "In your opinion based on what I'm sure is brilliant deduction."

Giles didn't respond for a moment. He needed more time to puzzle through the new information, but Willow's absent state indicated his earlier theory was correct.

"Justine has been participating in these community art festivals throughout the state," Giles said. "Three people have lapsed into comas and died in each town she's passed through in the past two months. Eighteen deaths plus four unfinished paintings equals twenty-two."

"Twenty-two what?" Buffy frowned, confused. "Deaths or paintings?"

"Both." Giles rose and began pacing, a habit that helped him to think. "If my assumptions are correct, and I believe they are, given their—" He gestured toward the catatonic crowd on the floor. "—condition, there are twenty-two Tarot paintings. The Major Arcana, to be more specific, which may explain Willow's reference to the 'new deck.' "

Buffy's eye flicked to the Tarot cards spread across the table. "That's the twenty-two power cards in the ancient Tarot, right?"

"Yes." Giles nodded, impressed with Buffy's recall. "I think Justine is empowering the paintings with the conscious essences of real people. Somehow she's managed to transfer her victims' emotional and mental processes."

Buffy straightened. "The Tarot readings."

"Most likely." Giles sighed. "For what purpose, I can't say just yet, but the victims slip into comatose states and die when the transfers are complete."

Willow stared, transfixed by the white lightning snapping around the gray stone tower visible beyond the transparent library wall. *So this is what it feels like to be in two places at once . . . mentally speaking.* The double-exposure factor made her nauseous.

Thunder rumbled through the fading library, drowning out the sound of Giles and Buffy's voices. The noise had kept her anchored, and she struggled to subdue a fresh surge of panic. Having an anxiety attack wouldn't help. Buffy and Giles now knew what was happening with Justine's paintings, and she had total confidence that the trusty librarian would also figure out why. *So I'm not going to let a little thing like having my mind drained into a horror film set get me down . . . yet.*

In that regard, staying mad would help a lot.

I've got a lot to be mad about, too, Willow thought defiantly. Xander hadn't faded out immediately after his reading. Neither had Oz, although he had lost touch faster than Xander. *So the whole steal-somebody's-brainwaves process must be speeding up, and that can't be good.*

Willow didn't want to dwell on the bad, which wasn't totally illogical . . . for a disembodied person watching screaming skeletons throw themselves off a massive stone tower in a demon-powered Tarot card. *Where I am but I'm not . . . thanks to Justine's magic deck.*

Willow had quickly figured out that the entrapment process had two insidious phases. Touching Justine's Tarot deck did a lot more than prime the cards for a specific reading. It created a psychic link that allowed the artist to take control of the subject's physical actions. The actual Tarot reading initiated the transfer of the subject's mental capacity into one of the paintings.

The reading had been interesting, though . . . aside from triggering the mind *whoosh*. She had been too busy adjusting to life inside a painting to really analyze all the subtle aspects revealed in the cards. Now seemed like a good time. The methodical exercise would keep her occupied, so she didn't turn into a deranged idiot before Buffy and Giles put her mind back where it belonged.

Although Willow knew she didn't have physical substance within the painting, it felt like she did. She perched on a rock and concentrated, trying to remember each Tarot card and Justine's interpretation.

Justine had dealt the Page of Swords first, which Willow knew was her personal Tarot ID for the reading. Even though she was female and not male, she did wear offbeat clothes and she *was* diplomatic and understanding . . . Even her rebellions—which were few and far between—were mild.

The Two of Swords was trickier to pinpoint, Willow mused. Based on her research, it indicated a tense relationship. The only relationship she could even remotely describe as being tense was with her parents. They saw her relationship with Buffy as a negative influence, and they were shocked to learn she was dating a musician. They didn't understand her, at all.

The next card was too on the mark, Willow thought uneasily. Judgment was a Major Arcana card. It was also the fourth and last of Justine's paintings— the one the artist hadn't found a victim for, yet.

Willow flinched when a lightning bolt cracked and struck nearby. A second strike sent an electrical shock through the ground and into her foot. "Ow!"

She stood up and jumped aside just before a third bolt turned the rock into melted slag. *This isn't real,* Willow reminded herself as a series of lightning strikes kept her moving toward the tower.

Willow didn't have a problem with being destined to blend her mind with the Universal as the Judgment card had indicated. However, being blended with a Tarot card was *not* the mind meld she would have chosen. Still, the accuracy of Justine's reading was eerie.

The cards that followed Judgment had sent conflicting messages; Ace of Cups for the beginning of a great love, while the Star combined spirit and an unconditional love.

Has to be Oz, Willow decided as she reached the base of the massive stone structure. The cut stones were huge and eroded. *Almost like they've been exposed to decades of acid rain,* she thought as she inspected the rough, crumbling surface.

Thunder rumbled in the distance. Willow turned to see a dark storm front rolling across a flat landscape. The ground in the wake of the driving rains turned to steaming liquid.

On the tower above her, a partially decomposed corpse screamed and plunged to the ground. Willow realized the effects of caustic rains and body bombs would not be pleasant, even if her corporeal form was merely a figment of her imagination. She scrambled around the base of the tower and ducked through a narrow opening into a dark, damp chamber with seconds to spare before the storm arrived.

Determined to stay steady and sane, Willow sat still in the dark. She forced her mind back to the Tarot reading, her only anchor in the surreal world of the Tower card.

The Six of Cups probably didn't have anything to do with Oz. The card foretold of new knowledge and opportunities. No problem there, but it also indicated that her happiness would come from things in the past. Willow was absolutely certain that everything that made her happy was in the present.

A spectacular barrage of lightning impacted on the tower. A web of pale blue and gold energies cascaded down the interior walls like a sparkling net.

Immediate circumstances excepted ... which I really don't want to dwell on.

The Major Arcana card Strength gave her some hope, though. It indicated that by refusing to give in to fear, she was using the "force of her character" to overcome a material enemy. At the moment, character didn't seem like a very effective weapon against the power of the artist's Tarot.

Justine the stupid or pathetically naïve, Willow thought with disgust, *who doesn't get that Kali wants to obliterate everything. Emphasis on* everything.

The stone walls vibrated as thunder boomed directly overhead, showering Willow in dust and debris. She shivered.

Willow frowned . . . or the equivalent of a virtual frown because she didn't really have a mouth, she just thought she did.

The Fool reflected what her family thought of her. *Translate that as parents—again. Are they right?* Willow wondered. *Are the decisions I've made thoughtless and bad?* She hadn't just been thinking of herself when she decided to delay early college admission. Buffy needed her right now . . . as a friend and an undaunted defender of good against evil. So did Giles and Xander and Oz!

Still, in reflection, Willow realized that leaving the Slayerettes behind would leave a gaping hole in her life. *What good is scientific success and a happy marriage—like the Sun card predicted—if the world is overrun by evil? Not a whole lot.*

Willow sighed. The Nine of Pentacles, the last card Justine dealt, had been ambiguous. Basically, a single decision would determine the course of her life for better or worse.

What decision?

Willow had no idea. It didn't matter now anyway. She couldn't do anything about any of the predictions until Buffy and Giles freed her from the Tarot trap. In the meantime, she would continue to resist the contagion of despair emanating from the depressing surroundings.

She listened to the storm rage outside the Tower and thought about Oz—both hers and the fictional land that had trapped a young girl from Kansas. Dorothy had made it home with a pair of red slippers and a simple mantra.

I've got the Slayer.

Buffy glanced at her three inert friends. *Soon-to-be-dead friends according to Giles. Not an option,* she thought with resolve. "Can we stop the mental downshift if we have the paintings?"

"I'm not sure." Giles stared at his notes, preoccupied with some fascinating fact Buffy hoped was a key to everyone's salvation. "Create fate . . . Perhaps, the new deck Justine is making may *determine* a person's destiny." Giles hesitated, as though the thought had just struck him. "Rather than simply predicting it."

"You mean Justine could design the future to order?" Buffy asked. "Just make anything happen that she wants to happen? Like deal-a-demon for fun?"

"Or profit." Giles wearily rubbed his eyes under his glasses. "If so, she would have the power to manipulate people and events at will once the painted deck is finished."

"But it's not finished—yet." Too agitated to sit still, Buffy slid off the chair.

"No, not until the last four paintings have been empowered. Presumably by Kali." Giles adjusted his glasses and leaned back with his hands behind his neck.

"Which won't happen until after Willow, Xander and Oz—" Buffy stumbled over the word, sickened by the thought.

"—are dead." Giles visibly balked, also unable to accept that outcome. He tapped his notes with his pen. "But we have time, Buffy. Not much, perhaps, but there must be a means of reversing the process. This word 'Hovan' might provide a key, if I can find a reference."

"Before Justine got to Willow, only two of her paintings had any color," Buffy said.

"The infusion of Xander and Oz's mental matrixes is responsible for the changes." Giles gave Buffy a pointed look. "We have to retrieve all of the paintings Justine has in her motel room."

"And not because you want to brighten up the library walls."

"Hardly." Giles sighed. "Two reasons, actually. I suspect we'll need the paintings to retrieve Xander, Willow, and Oz's minds once I've deduced how. Then, assuming Willow's mind is empowering the third Tarot painting—"

"There's still a fourth!" Buffy jumped up. "If we have it, Justine won't be able to finish the deck."

Giles glanced at his watch. "Unless we're too late and she's already found a donor."

"On my way." Buffy fished Oz's car keys out of his pocket and frowned when Giles looked at her askance. "I may be the Slayer, but I can't carry four huge paintings back here from the motel. Oz's van is probably still parked outside Justine's room."

"Yes, well . . . be careful. At least, there's not much traffic this time of night."

"I'll take the back roads," Buffy solemnly promised.

"Make absolutely certain no harm comes to the paintings," Giles warned. "The empowering essences might be damaged or destroyed with them."

Turning my friends into mindless vegetables, Buffy thought, *if they survive.*

Buffy maintained a steady jog on her way across town. She had been back and forth to the Golden Lantern Motel so many times now her feet had memorized the route. Lulled by the steady rhythm of her stride, her thoughts settled on her friends and their predicament, which they wouldn't be in if it weren't for their loyalty to her. The thought grated on Buffy's conscience. If after graduation they stayed in Sunnydale to fight by her side, they'd always be in constant danger.

If they survived the Tarot threat, Buffy would urge them to leave and follow their dreams after graduation. *Before it's too late . . . .*

Since Willow, Xander, and Oz were all incapacitated, Buffy and Giles would have to figure out Justine's game plan and how to stop her by themselves. Cordelia had stopped volunteering for active demon duty after her breakup with Xander and Anya didn't care about anything *except* Xander. Saving him might rally the ex-demon to fight, but that's as far as her motives could be trusted. Buffy didn't want to take the chance Anya would barter with Kali: Xander's life in exchange for everything and everyone else.

So it's up to Giles and me. That was how the system had worked for centuries, though: a Slayer and her Watcher working together against the forces of darkness. That hadn't changed just because the Watchers Council had fired Giles. Her friends were an invaluable asset, to be sure, but she and Giles could handle this gig solo.

The dark streets were quiet now that the clubs had closed. As far as Buffy knew, Justine thought Sunnydale was just another sleepy small town with no defense against her mind-robbing Tarot deck. Certainly, the artist didn't know that a vampire Slayer with enhanced physical powers and senses was aware of her murderous activities. Still, Buffy broke into a run, anxious to get to the motel and secure the paintings. On the Hellmouth, nothing could be taken for granted.

A shrill scream sounded from a twenty-four–hour gas station mini-mart two blocks from the Golden Lantern. Pulling her stake, Buffy automatically darted toward the complex at the intersection, assessing the situation as she charged to the rescue.

Rob Chambers huddled behind a display case that had been dragged in front of the doors. Cordelia was searching the store for weapons. Everyone else had taken cover. A woman shrieked when the monsters broke a window.

A fourth vamp, wearing a greasy, mechanic's coverall, dropped the body of a woman by the gas pumps when he saw Buffy barreling toward him. Snarling and roaring, the spindly demon raced to meet her head-on.

Either too new or too retarded to recognize a fatal pointy thing when he sees it, Buffy thought, running with her stake raised. A split second before the undead beanpole could meet his destiny on the wooden spike he leaped to the side.

Buffy whirled to face him, spread her arms, and smiled. "You want to dance? Here I am."

Yellow eyes glittered under the ridged vampire brow and fangs gleamed when he grinned. "I don't dance."

"Neither do I." Spring-coiled, Buffy rushed and ducked under the long arms the not-too-bright vamp tried to throw around her. A swift kick knocked his legs out from under him and her stake plunged into his heart before he hit the ground. "Not with undead freaks anyway."

Buffy was off across the parking lot before the dust cloud cleared. The vampire trio was so intent on storming into the store through the shattered windows they didn't hear her coming. She leaped in after them and joined a free-for-all of fangs and fists.

The teenaged cashier, a jogger—*obviously an out-of-towner,* she thought—and a cowboy in jeans, western hat, and boots, were fending off one of the vamps by the counter. A teenaged girl hurled canned goods at a second vamp and squealed in short, staccato bursts. A squat, round vampire stood between Buffy and the brawl, staring down an elderly woman in a straw hat with a handbag dangling on her arm.

Like he can't quite make up his mind if he wants aged or freshly brewed, Buffy thought with a quick glance at the girl. The vamp in a grungy business suit caught one of her cans and threw it back. She ducked, still squealing.

The three men by the counter were clinging to the younger, brawnier fanged menace who spun trying to shake them off.

Rob stared at the scene in wide-eyed horror. Cordelia had disappeared.

Okay, Buffy thought, tightening her grip on her stake. *Show's over.*

When the short vamp snarled and grabbed at the old woman, Buffy closed the distance in two strides. The woman screamed and clamped her eyes shut just before Buffy landed a swift kick to the vamp's rib cage. He staggered into the aisle display shelves. Cereal boxes and assorted jars smashed on the floor.

As Buffy raised her stake to finish him off the hysterical old lady bashed her over the head with her handbag.

"Go away! Go away!"

"When I'm finished." Buffy yanked the purse free and tossed it over her shoulder.

The girl's steady stream of squeals became a high-pitched scream when Suit Vamp lunged toward her.

Cordelia ran out of a back room carrying a broom and whacked the vamp in the business suit over the head. The blow had no effect except to divert the demon's attention from the girl to Cordy. "You guys really know how to spoil a perfect evening."

The short vamp recovered and tackled Buffy around the legs. Keeping her grip on the stake, Buffy flipped the vamp as she fell backward. He dove into another display, knocking it over. Up and on her feet instantly, Buffy staked the dazed vampire on the rebound. "That's one vamp with a short shelf life."

"Back off, Biz Boy." Holding the broom like a spear to keep Suit Vamp at bay, Cordelia turned her scathing glance on the screaming girl. "Will you please shut up?"

The girl kept screaming as Suit Vamp snatched the broom out of Cordelia's hands and snapped the handle in half.

"Now look what you did!" Cordy glared at the snarling demon and grabbed one of the broken shafts back. When the vamp attacked, she plunged the pointy end into his chest. "Thanks."

The girl watched the vamp disintegrate, then passed out herself.

"Incoming!" Cordelia yelled as Buffy leaped past the shocked grandmother.

Buffy ducked the flying cowboy the large vamp threw across the store like a rag doll.

Cordelia tucked her broom handle under her arm and walked over to Rob, who was still cowering by the display case barricade. "This little disturbance isn't going to affect your review of the art show, is it?"

At the counter, the cashier and the jogger struggled to free themselves from the large vamp's grip on their collars.

Buffy dashed to the front of the store. Her stake thwacked into the large vamp's back just before his fangs sank into the jogger's neck. Then she sprang through the broken window without breaking stride or looking back. She didn't have time to answer questions or calm shattered nerves. The undead were up and about town prowling for prey. As soon as she got Justine's paintings back to Giles, she had to patrol.

The Golden Lantern Motel parking lot was full of vans and cars. Visiting artists were tucked in and safe from undead intruders. Buffy's relief was only momentary, though. Oz's van sat outside the end unit, but the dragon-mobile was absent. Unable to see into the room through the darkened window, Buffy slammed against the door, breaking the lock.

She burst inside ready for a fight and flicked on the light.

Justine, her belongings, and the paintings were gone.

"Now what?" Buffy's eye traveled to the phone on the nightstand. *When in doubt, call Giles.*

Giles was silent for a moment after she explained that Justine's room was empty. "I doubt she's gone . . . from Sunnydale, that is. Or perhaps I should say, from the Hellmouth."

Buffy hesitated, stricken by a chilling dread of the underworld portal. Her voice was tight when she spoke. "How does the Hellmouth fit into this?"

"Kali." Giles sighed. "I haven't confirmed anything yet, but it's entirely reasonable to assume the goddess must be present to empower the paintings when Justine finishes the deck."

Buffy nodded. "Makes sense. Let's just hope Justine hasn't found a mind to transfer into painting number four."

"Yes, that would probably be disastrous," Giles agreed. "You must locate those paintings before Justine initiates the final phase."

"I'm out of here." With Oz's keys in hand, Buffy left and got into the van. She could cover more territory patrolling on wheels, even though it would cut down her response time. *Nothing I can do about that.* The vampire threat seemed tame compared to a Tarot deck that would allow Justine to manipulate the future at will.

Easing the van into gear, Buffy pulled slowly out of the parking lot onto the empty street and headed toward the mansion to find Angel. The dragon-mobile was easy to spot, but there were hundreds of places Justine could hole up in Sunnydale. Scouting the hotels, motels, warehouses, and underground system of tunnels and pipes to find the artist wouldn't be a problem.

If we had a week.

CHAPTER 11

A dozen artists were waiting for Joyce when she arrived at the gallery before the festival opened Saturday morning. The collective mood was angry and frightened.

Not a surprise, Joyce thought as she shoved through the crowd to open the gallery. According to the morning newspaper, two artists had been killed the night before—by muggers. The police department had received several calls reporting break-ins and violent disturbances. The two deaths were tragic, but Joyce knew that the situation would have been much worse if Buffy hadn't been out patrolling. Not even the Slayer could be expected to be everywhere at once.

"I want a refund." An older gentleman with a beard stormed inside on Joyce's heels.

"Me, too," a woman's shrill voice added. "I'm not staying in any town that can't keep its streets safe for law-abiding citizens."

"I'm from Ridgecrest," another man piped up. "We haven't had a crime wave since the Gold Rush a hundred and fifty years ago. I want to be gone within the hour."

"Yes, well—why don't I make some coffee, while you all take a moment to calm down. I'm sure we can work something out." Joyce smiled and fled toward her office, wishing Willow hadn't picked today to be late. She turned on the large, restaurant-style coffee maker sitting on the table outside the door.

Darting inside, Joyce closed the door to shut out the grumbling artists milling about the showroom and picked up the phone. Buffy hadn't come home last night and there was still no answer at their house. Joyce kept a tight rein on her anxiety. She tried to tell herself that Buffy was probably in the shower or on her way into town with Willow.

After downing a half-full mug of maximum-strength coffee, Joyce took a deep breath. Fortified, she left to try and save what might be the last Sunny-dale Sidewalk Art Festival. She coaxed the distraught artists into an orderly line and sat at the computer to handle their complaints one by one. An hour later, all but three had decided to stay—at least through the Saturday portion of the weekend event. That was one worry tabled for the day, but another quickly replaced it.

Willow and Buffy had not shown up.

"Giles?" Back in her office, Joyce tightened her grip on the receiver. Buffy was not in the habit of checking in as regularly as Joyce would have liked now that she knew the nature of her daughter's extracurricular activities. Usually, she managed to control her mother-hen impulses, but sometimes the maternal instinct was stronger than protecting Buffy's adult self-image.

"I'm fine, thank you," Joyce said. "Are Buffy and Willow there? The art show's about to open and I need Willow on hand in the gallery."

"Actually, I, uh . . . saw Willow . . . earlier." Giles cleared his throat. "Something unexpected came up and she won't be able to make it."

"Is something wrong?" Joyce tensed. "Is Buffy all right?"

"Buffy's fine," Giles interjected. "She was patrolling most of the night. Perhaps she turned off the ringer to sleep."

"Oh, she probably did." Joyce sagged, feeling foolish as she hung up. Buffy needed to sleep undisturbed if she was going to patrol again at sundown. "Now all I need is someone to watch the shop—"

"Is Xander here?" Buffy's strange friend—Anya, if Joyce recalled correctly—barged into the office and confronted her as though she was the keeper of Xander's date book.

"I haven't seen him today." Come to think of it, Joyce hadn't seen Xander yesterday, either, but she hadn't really expected him. His volunteer services hadn't been needed once the artists had finished setting up. She suspected Xander was just avoiding the brazen young woman.

"He's missing," Anya announced darkly.

"He's not missing," Cordelia said as she strolled in. "He left last night."

"For where?" Anya demanded.

"L.A. Where else?" Cordelia fixed Joyce with a cocked eyebrow. "I wouldn't count on a good review in *California Art* magazine."

Joyce raised an eyebrow at Cordelia. "You're talking about the reporter, Rob Chambers? How can he write a review when the show just started?"

"A close encounter with a few fanged punks in the mini-mart probably had something to do with it." Cordelia rolled her eyes. "That guy has a rubber backbone."

"I see." Joyce sighed.

"And *no* sense of professional obligation. I spend two whole days showing that creep the dim, but brighter side of life in Sunnydale, and he takes off without even asking for my phone number!" Cordelia threw up her hands. "You can't have too many contacts in L.A., you know."

"What does that have to do with Xander?" Anya asked.

"Absolutely nothing." Cordelia paused at the door on her way out. "A word of advice, Anya. Getting too close to Xander will be hazardous to your health."

"Not your fault, Cordelia." Joyce sighed and closed her eyes after Cordelia left. A long moment passed before she remembered Anya. The young woman was staring at her. "I'll tell Xander you're looking for him, Anya, if I see him."

"I'll just wait." Anya leaned against the wall and folded her arms.

"Here? But—" Joyce didn't know Anya very well, but she needed someone to watch the gallery while she circulated through the art show. Some high-powered damage control was essential or the remaining artists wouldn't survive the weekend. "Then would you mind answering the phone and taking messages? Just until Xander shows up—or I get back."

"Might as well." Anya shrugged. Her eyes narrowed. "If I don't keep busy I might strangle the next man I see."

"Your mother called this morning. Have you spoken to her?" Giles shoved a pile of books aside to make room for Buffy and her take-out bag at the study table.

"I left a message on the gallery answering machine. Mom must have run out of volunteers." Buffy popped the plastic lid off a steaming cup of coffee and blew on it. She had patrolled until just before dawn and needed the caffeine jump-start even though she had slept for a solid two hours. Even a Slayer couldn't keep going indefinitely without sleep.

"That would seem to be the case. She called looking for you and Willow." Giles glanced over his shoulder. Willow and Oz sat at rigid attention. Xander was stretched out on the floor. "I told her Willow was . . . busy."

Buffy unwrapped an English muffin stuffed with sausage.

"What is that?" Giles recoiled slightly.

"Breakfast."

Giles looked appalled.

Buffy shrugged. "I can't cope with failure on an empty stomach. I didn't find the paintings."

Although she had sent a dozen undead troublemakers to the happy dusting grounds, there was no trace of Justine or the Tarot paintings. She and Angel had covered a lot of territory, but without a lead, a thorough search of the extensive warehouse district and underground network just hadn't been possible.

Frustrated and worried, Buffy looked at her friends. "How long have they been like that?"

"Hours," Giles said. "Oz and Willow slept for a while."

"How could you tell?"

"They closed their eyes." Sighing, Giles avoided looking at his temporary roommates. "Xander slipped into a coma sometime during the night."

The muffin lodged in Buffy's throat. She forced it down. "How long does he have left?"

"A matter of hours." Giles shuffled through his notes. "The absorption process seems to be accelerated in Oz and Willow. They're declining much faster than Xander. There is good news, though—if you want to call it that."

Buffy frowned. "That bad, huh?"

"That depends, actually." Giles shifted in his seat. "I found a fairly detailed account about Hovan Ramos in an old monastery text. His notes were never found, but he confided in a monk who was sympathetic to the plight of the Romani."

Buffy ate and listened as Giles explained. Hovan had created Justine's Tarot deck, which had been empowered by Kali at a European site similar to the Hellmouth six centuries ago. The deck allowed Justine to take control of an individual's mind and transfer the mental and emotional energies into the paintings.

"Hovan resented the persecution of the Gypsies," Giles said, "and planned to use the deck to elevate his people to positions of power, wealth, and respect."

"Which didn't happen." Buffy stuffed her litter into the bag and set it aside. "Why not?"

"Because he realized that keeping his bargain with Kali would be cataclysmic." Giles eyed Buffy pointedly. "She wanted 'perfect order' in exchange for her help."

"A little peace and quiet would be a relief."

A wry smile softened Giles's grim expression. "No doubt, but as I explained to Willow, *perfect* order is not possible until *everything* is eliminated— beginning with free will and ending when the universe ceases to exist."

"When there's nothing left but . . . nothing?" Buffy's eyes widened.

Giles nodded. "Kali will have achieved her cosmic purpose when the universe is a complete void. If events progress naturally, she cannot escape the underworld until the end is imminent several billion years in the future."

"And she's getting tired of waiting, right?" Buffy arched an eyebrow.

"Yes, apparently." Giles leaned over a dusty tome that was open on the table. "Hovan deduced that once Kali's Major Arcana deck was finished—"

"The paintings," Buffy interjected for clarification.

"Yes, the paintings." Giles adjusted his glasses and went on. "When all twenty-two have absorbed a psyche, the deck can be used, as I surmised earlier, to *determine* rather than predict the future. Hovan figured out that Kali had no intention of honoring her part of their pact. She planned to subvert his free will to her own, then use the psyche-powered Major Arcana to accelerate the destructive process."

Buffy blinked. "Huh?"

"Use the empowered Tarot paintings to speed up the end of the universe." Giles looked up. "By several billion years."

"And I thought *I* was impatient."

"Unfortunately, so is Justine." Agitated, Giles sipped his tea and grimaced. "Cold. Anyhow, I suspect her art show itinerary was calculated to conclude in Sunnydale . . . near the Hellmouth. Although Kali cannot physically breach the Hell-mouth's weak barrier between this world and the underworld, she is quite capable of projecting her will onto Justine. Just as she empowered the Hovan deck Justine uses to snare her victims."

Buffy paused, stricken by the implication. "So Kali's original plan to make nothing out of everything has only been delayed for six hundred years."

"I'm afraid so." Giles leaned back and sighed.

"But I don't have 'universe ends' penciled into my organizer." Buffy joked to mask her anxiety. Stopping diabolical plots to end the world had almost become routine. Keeping the *universe* up and running wasn't how she had planned to spend the weekend.

Giles smiled. "Not an everyday occurrence, even on the Hellmouth."

Buffy sat bolt upright. "Justine doesn't know!"

"Come again?" Giles started.

"Justine doesn't know that *Kali* will be in control of her mind and the doomsday deck!" Buffy jumped up. "Justine is sinister and selfish, but she's not stupid enough to let some goddess with a bad rep take over her brain. She's after glory."

"Yes, that goes without saying."

"Oh." Buffy frowned, annoyed.

"Not that it wasn't an astute observation," Giles added. "It was quite . . . astute." He quickly turned his attention back to the book. "This reference concerning the Judgment card is rather disturbing."

The mention of Justine's final Tarot painting

jarred Buffy. She still had to find the paintings to stop Justine from completing Kali's deck. She scooped up the remains of her breakfast to toss them in the trash.

" 'The battleground where good must prevail,' " Giles muttered.

"Prevail." Buffy stopped halfway into the office. "So it's possible to win? From inside the painting?"

"That's the logical interpretation." Giles flipped off his glasses. "I suppose it will depend on the emotional strength of the last donor. Hopefully, Justine hasn't initiated the final transfer, yet."

Buffy wasn't thinking about an unknown fourth victim. She looked at Xander lying comatose on the floor, at Willow and Oz sitting like stone statues. All of them were on a one-way trip to the cemetery—and *not* to help her patrol. "What about getting them out?"

Dust wafted into the air as Giles turned the pages in the book. "This passage is somewhat vague, but it suggests that the captive minds might escape if the paintings are destroyed before the transfer processes are complete and the last card is empowered."

"Then I'm going to find them." Buffy lobbed the bag into the wastepaper basket by Giles' desk and turned to leave.

"Wait—" Giles' sharp tone brought the Slayer to a lurching halt. "I think it would be prudent to try and narrow the realm of your search . . . rather than blindly stumbling about."

Buffy couldn't argue that after her fruitless efforts

last night. "I'll call my mom to see if Justine showed up at her display. If not, she can keep an eye out."

"Yes, good, but . . . there's another catch."

"There always is." Buffy returned to the table and sat back down.

"Xander, Willow, and Oz must be physically present when the paintings are destroyed," Giles said. "If the bodies aren't in proximity to the pieces when their mental essences are released, the energies will simply dissipate."

"Good to know. Is that the last ax in your bad news arsenal or is there more? Such as, can we still stop Kali if Justine finishes the Major Arcana deck?"

"No." Giles's blunt response sent a chill up Buffy's spine. "When Kali's deck is completed, Justine, acting as the dark goddess directs, can seal the fate of anyone—even kill a Slayer—just by dealing the cards."

CHAPTER 12

Playing gallery secretary had gotten old fast. When Anya had stepped outside and missed a call, the answering machine had picked up. After that, she let the technological marvel handle the duty while she worried.

About Xander.

No one had seen him in two days!

Is Xander avoiding everyone, or did he run off with that woman? Or has something bad happened to him? All of the above? None of the above?

Anya paced back and forth in front of the registration table. Joyce hadn't been back for hours and she was tired of being stuck. She had thought about just walking out, then decided against it. If something turned up missing or broken because she had left the gallery unattended, Buffy's mom would blame her. Not that she cared, but defending herself would be more trouble then hanging out awhile longer.

"Hello, dear," a cheerful voice said.

Anya whirled to see an elderly woman enter carrying a cardboard box. Smiling, the gray-haired woman stooped to shove it under the registration table.

"There you go." The woman put a hand on her bowed back as she straightened up. The box contained neat piles of brightly colored ribbons with gold lettering. "Arthur's Trophy Shop did quite a nice job on the awards, didn't they?"

"Terrific." Anya had no idea what she was talking about and didn't care. Joyce didn't care what live body was watching the store as long as someone was. The woman was breathing, which qualified her for taking over the boring task. Anya grabbed the chance to escape and hurried toward the door. "I'm late. Gotta go!"

"But—but I'm not supposed to *stay* here!" The old woman started after her, waving frantically.

Anya bolted down the street leaving the flustered woman standing in the gallery doorway. The crackers and cheese she had found in Joyce's small office refrigerator had taken the edge off at noon, but now she was suddenly famished.

Acute anxiety always makes me hungry, Anya thought as she ducked into a small restaurant that specialized in chicken. She slipped into a booth by the window and stared out at the Saturday crowd browsing through the displays. Xander was out there somewhere. *Where?* Frustrated, she struck the table with her fist.

The waitress inhaled sharply. Her voice squeaked when she spoke. "Something to drink?"

"Iced tea and a broiled chicken sandwich." Anya sagged when the woman fled. She felt rotten, like someone had put her heart in a vise and squeezed the life out of it. Falling in love was a design flaw in the human species she could happily have done without.

Xander had made it clear that he wasn't interested in pursuing a romance with her, but he knew what she had been and accepted it—to a degree. He also understood that adjusting to being human and learning the social dos and don'ts was hard! She actually appreciated his brutal honesty when he was talking to her, which he currently wasn't.

Anya sighed, propped her chin, and stared out the window. Feeling sorry for herself aggravated the hunger that twisted her stomach. Anger was so much more satisfying than angst, but neither emotion was accomplishing anything.

There was, she realized, only one thing that would soothe the ache in her wretchedly human heart. As soon as she finished her late lunch she was going to keep looking for Xander until she found him and settled things once and for all.

Whether he likes it or not, Xander is mine!

Justine flicked on her flashlight and scanned the underground cavern. It was dimly lit by several camp lanterns. The only sound was the drip of water that seeped from the rock and overflowing natural catch basins eroded into the rough walls. Patches of phosphorescent lichen and spongy mosses softened the hard stone surface, creating an ambience of eerie foreboding that suited her plans. The cave was damp and uncomfortable, but she only had to stay one more night.

Kali's destiny deck would be finished before dawn. *And tomorrow the world will be mine,* Justine thought as she turned off the lamps.

A card table and two folding chairs dominated the center under the high, domed ceiling. A cot covered with a sleeping bag stood against one wall beside an overturned crate. A lamp and battery-operated clock sat on the makeshift nightstand. The paintings were lined up along the far wall.

Justine paused to study them. The eighteen pieces she had finished before arriving in Sunnydale shimmered with the life forces imprisoned within them. The final four paintings remained in various stages of progress. They would not be complete until the last card, Judgment, absorbed the emotional essences of her final victim. All four of the powerful Major Arcana cards would be empowered in the same instant. *Then nothing can stop me from doing or having anything I want.*

After turning off the last light, Justine used the flashlight to lead her to the narrow entrance. Guided by a Tarot reading, she had come to Sunnydale several months before. The cards had left nothing to chance. Sunnydale had to be the last stop on her bizarre journey and the grand finale had to take place underground. She had explored the maze under Sunnydale for days before she finally found the crevice that led to the hidden cavern.

When Justine exited the natural corridor that connected the cave to a network of man-made tunnels, she turned off the flashlight and set it on a broken timber. Permanent light fixtures were spaced along the route to the exit. Only half the bulbs were burning, but the power was always on. Apparently, city maintenance crews still used the submerged access way. Consequently, she moved warily just in case someone came down to fix a broken water pipe or junction box.

She didn't need any surprises, not when she was this close or this tense. She had experienced some apprehension since the last Tarot reading had revealed the only obstacle in her way—the Queen of Wands. Justine had no doubt that Buffy Summers was the blond woman who would determine whether she succeeded or failed.

She had no intention of failing.

Justine paused when she reached the ladder under a trap door, which opened into the basement of an old, vacant building on the perimeter of the downtown area. A back door on the ground floor opened into an alley. Once she controlled Buffy's mind and actions, it would be easy to slip away unseen.

Justine smiled, pleased with her solution to the

Queen of Wands problem. The unknown threat Buffy presented would be neutralized when she touched Hovan's deck. Even better, Buffy's dynamic personality would empower the last, most powerful card—the Judgment painting. Once again, the Tarot indicators and her interpretation had been accurate. Free will had determined how she would act to turn a potential problem into an asset. She didn't expect any trouble.

Willow's remarkable resistance had been a fluke. In retrospect, Justine wished she hadn't chosen Xander for her first Sunnydale subject. In every other town, the friends and families of the donors had rushed the victims to psychologists when they began to disassociate or into hospitals when they became comatose. Of course, the transfer process took a lot longer in the beginning, and she had been long gone by the time the maladies became apparent. She had had no way of knowing that Xander's best friends would make a connection between her and his condition and start investigating! Their tenacious curiosity had shaken her at first. Then she had realized that using Oz, Willow, and Buffy for the remaining three cards was the best and safest way to eliminate the interference.

Justine climbed into the basement and hurried up the staircase to the first floor. She peeked through a grimy window to make sure no one was lurking in the alley, then darted through the door. Once outside, she took Hovan's deck out of her pocket and palmed it. When she found Buffy, she could easily shove it into Buffy's hand before she knew what was happening.

And then she won't be able to do anything without a direct order from me.

Taking a deep breath, Justine casually walked out of the alley and surveyed the busy street. Hundreds of people were wandering the streets, browsing the artists' displays. Finding one blond woman in the crowd wasn't going to be easy. *Unless Buffy is looking for me!* That was entirely possible, since her friends were steadily declining into comas.

Justine turned to walk toward her own display, the most likely place Buffy would go to find her. If she didn't find her there, the next logical spot to check was her mother's art gallery.

The milling crowd jammed the sidewalk, forcing Justine into the cordoned-off street. Her pace was slowed by having to weave around parents pushing baby strollers or chasing unruly toddlers. Elderly couples took their time, while teens on Roller Blades whizzed by. Irritated and distracted, she didn't see Xander's friend Anya until the woman was on top of her.

"Where's Xander?" The young woman's chest heaved with barely contained fury.

Justine frowned, recalling the woman's rude remarks to the reporter the first night of the art show. She had questioned Xander to find that he wasn't particularly fond of the woman, either.

"Anya, also known as bad news for boys," Xander had said.

"Sorry. I don't know." Annoyed by the delay, Justine tried to move on.

"Wait! I just want to know where—" When Anya's hand flashed out to grab her, Justine instinctively raised her arm. Anya's fingers closed around her hand—and Hovan's deck.

"No!" Justine gasped as Anya froze, her mind captured by the power of the enchanted cards. Stunned, Justine just stared for a moment. She did not know how to undo the spell or even if it could be undone. On a freak quirk of fate, she would have to use this miserable girl to empower the last painting—not Buffy.

Suddenly anxious, Justine glanced around the crowded street. Buffy was nowhere in sight, which was a huge stroke of luck. Once she got Anya underground, the dangerous Queen of Wands wouldn't be a threat. Buffy couldn't interfere with the final stage if she didn't know where they were.

"Follow me." Justine turned and headed back toward the alley.

Anya fell into step behind her.

CHAPTER 13

Joyce disconnected her cell phone when she saw Anya shoving her way through the crowd across the street. She was already upset because the answering machine was picking up calls, but she hadn't expected Anya to actually leave the gallery unattended.

"Anya!" Joyce shouted, but the girl didn't hear her. *Or doesn't want to! And I don't need something else to worry about.*

Joyce eased into the flow of the art show browsers to chase Anya down. Buffy had called from the library half an hour ago asking about Justine. For reasons her daughter wouldn't explain—again—it was urgent that she and Giles find the artist. Coming from Buffy, urgent usually meant some kind of catastrophic chaos was about to erupt. Joyce hadn't seen

Justine all day, but had promised to look for her and report her location if she found her. However, she couldn't search the art show if the gallery was empty. With luck, Anya had left someone else in charge.

"Anya!" Joyce jumped and waved, but Anya was barreling through the throng like a runaway locomotive.

Joyce kept going until a knot of people watching a street magician blocked her path. Holding her temper, she worked her way around the blockade. Anya had stopped moving several yards away and was talking to someone. Joyce started to shout again, then realized the other person was the artist Justine. Both women suddenly turned and started walking away from her.

Following, Joyce got out her cell phone and dialed Giles' office while keeping Justine and Anya in sight. Anya was apparently part of the unknown disaster that was about to befall the town. After all they'd been through, Joyce knew that getting word to Buffy the Slayer and her trusty Watcher was more imperative than protecting the gallery from light-fingered art lovers.

"Giles! It's Joyce." Joyce put a finger in her ear.

"Have you located Justine?" Giles asked.

"Yes. She's at the art show with Anya. Wait a minute—" Joyce lost sight of them and elbowed her way forward.

"Anya? What is Anya—" Giles hesitated. "Is she acting strangely by any chance?"

"I can't see—" Joyce cleared the crowd and spotted the two women on the sidewalk. "Strangely? I don't think so. She and Justine just went into the alley between Wooden Wares and the old Fabrics and Notions."

"Alley by Wooden Wares and Fabrics and Notions." Giles voice sounded distant and clipped.

"I know where it is." Joyce heard Buffy in the background.

"The fabric store went out of business six months ago," Joyce added. "Does that help?"

"Yes, very much. Thank you. Can you keep them in sight without being seen?" Giles asked. "We don't want to lose them, but you must be careful."

"I'm moving as we speak. Hang on. Is something going on?" Keeping the line open, Joyce hopped the curb and cautiously approached the alley. Afternoon shadows had begun to darken the narrow corridor. The deserted fabric store seemed like an island of gloom in the midst of the festival. Breathing in deeply, she raised the phone to her ear and peeked around the corner. "The alley's a dead end, Giles, but—they're gone!"

"We're on our way."

"Should I—" Joyce started when the phone went dead in her hand.

"There's a trap door in the basement of that old sewing store that leads to the city tunnels," Buffy said when Giles hung up. "And a thousand places Justine could be hiding down there!"

"Yes, but she doesn't know her way around the underground network." Although Buffy was quite correct, Giles maintained an outward calm. "Chances are she's chosen an access that's relatively close to her hiding place. Less risk of getting lost."

"We can hope anyway." Buffy frowned.

"You go on ahead." Giles pointed to the door, then glanced back over his shoulder. Willow and Oz had slumped forward and Xander was still stretched out on the floor. "I'll have to transport Xander, Willow and Oz myself somehow."

"*How* is the problem, isn't it?" Buffy hesitated. "I think I'd better help. They have to be there when I destroy the paintings or they'll die."

Giles spoke as he moved toward the comatose trio. "No, Justine must not finish Anya's Tarot reading or the last painting will be empowered. If Kali's essence emerges and lodges in Justine's mind, then *all* is lost. Go!"

"Out of here." Buffy raced through the doors and was gone.

Giles turned his attention to the three mentally deactivated young people. Over the past three years they had gone from being a pleasant but unsettling inconvenience who threatened the Slayer's secret and mission to being indispensable associates and friends. He would get them to Justine's location if he had to carry them one at a time.

"That should be the last resort, however," Giles muttered as he positioned himself in front of Willow and Oz. He felt ridiculous commanding the almost mindless bodies, but he hardly had a choice. "Stand up."

To his immense relief, they both rose. Sluggishly, but they were on their feet and still responding to spoken commands. After shoving his car keys into his pocket, Giles ordered Oz to lift and brace Xander on one side while he took the other. With Willow moving ahead to open and close doors per his precise instructions, Giles and Oz propped up and dragged the comatose Xander to Oz's van.

Anya fought the hold Justine had on her mind without success. All the determined anger she could muster had no effect on muscles and limbs that were bound by the artist's command. She stopped trying as she climbed down the ladder into the tunnel under the deserted store. The only thing that kept the futility of her circumstances from driving her insane was the hope that Justine would lead her to Xander.

He might be down here, too, Anya told herself. *In fact, Justine probably used this weird whammy to make him do what* she *wanted!*

The idea that the artist had *forced* Xander's attention away from her lifted Anya's spirits and gave her courage. It also gave her purpose.

Justine hadn't turned her into a puppet for fun. Whatever the artist had planned for her and Xander had to be of the bad . . . as Buffy liked to say.

Buffy!

Hope jarred Anya as her feet touched hard ground. The Slayer got on her nerves a lot, especially since Xander liked to spend so much time with her. However, Buffy wouldn't ignore a missing friend. She and the stuffy librarian would search every inch of Sunnydale to find him, including the labyrinth of tunnels and caves.

"This way!" Justine barked.

Anya turned to follow like a cowed cur. *Do something! You can't be coerced by a lower magician! It's embarassing!* Desperate, she tried to resist again. Her legs stubbornly moved after the artist, but the force of Anya's indignation affected her gait. Her foot dragged, digging a long depression in the dust.

Not terribly effective, Anya thought, *but better than meeting some horrible fate without trying to fight back.* Considering that she had been responsible for a fair measure of horrible fates over the centuries, the irony of being shanghaied into Justine's unknown, but no doubt diabolical plan was not lost on her. She wasn't about to make things any easier on the artist than necessary.

Anya fought her legs with every stride as Justine drove deeper and deeper into the tunnel system. There wasn't much chance that Buffy would find this exact location anytime soon, but it was the only chance she had. Behind her, she left a trail of long marks.

* * *

Joyce was still hanging out in front of Wooden Wares. Her worried look intensified as Buffy approached. "What's going on, Buffy?"

"Nothing much," Buffy quipped. "Just a little problem with the continued existence of the universe."

"The *whole* universe?" Joyce gasped.

"Yeah. We've upgraded from saving the world." Buffy called back as she ran toward the door leading into the vacant fabric store. "You can go now, Mom. I can take things from here."

"Where's Giles?" Joyce called back.

"He's on his way!" Buffy tried the doorknob. It was locked from the inside, but the old bolt gave easily when she threw her weight against the door. She paused just long enough to watch her mother leave, then rushed inside and down the rickety stairs to the basement. She had found the trap door during a mad dash to escape a particularly durable demon last year, but had not used it again. The tunnels below were tributaries of the main network and connected to a series of caves and caverns.

And about a hundred of them would be a perfect hangout for a mad artist who wants privacy!

Buffy jumped off the ladder and stopped to listen. There was nothing to hear except the rustling of foraging rats. About twenty minutes had passed since her mother had called, which gave Justine a decent head start even with Anya stuck in robot gear. Some of the lights in the secondary maintenance access tunnel were working. That would make moving through the maze easier, but wouldn't help her find Justine.

Or would it?

Buffy scanned the floor. The dust and dirt around the base of the ladder was imprinted with a jumble of footprints. Some of the prints disappeared into the tunnel on the left, but the fresher, smaller ones had been coming and going from the right. A long, narrow mark caught her eye when she reached across it to pick up stones and broken pieces of wood from a pile against the wall. Confident about the direction Justine had taken, she constructed a rough arrow for Giles to follow, then headed down the passageway.

She kept her eye on the prints, but the layer of dust became thinner and nonexistent in places as she got farther from the entrance. It became difficult to distinguish the old from the new and the smaller from the larger. The tunnel shaft was made from rock shored up with occasional rusty metal plates and timbers. She stopped every fifty feet or so to make another pointer, hoping the British born and raised Giles had enough pioneer savvy to recognize them as direction markers.

When Buffy came to the first break in the stone that was wide enough for a person to squeeze through, she checked for prints.

No footprints pointed into the dark break, but her gaze focused on a long, deep mark in the dust.

Buffy knelt to study it closer. There was nothing remarkable about the depression—except that it was identical to the mark by the ladder and unmarred by an overlying footprint. *Fresh?* Curious, Buffy glanced to each side and realized the marks ran as far as she could see along the tunnel floor. The toe of the shoe was clearly squared off.

Anya?

Like Willow, Buffy wasn't quite sure how she felt about the newly-human woman who had spent the last thousand years making men miserable. She didn't have a problem with Anya's bluntly honest approach to everything because there was never a question about how she felt or what she thought. In fact, the only thing she seemed to think about was Xander.

Buffy frowned. Last night Anya had assumed Xander was with Justine. Since Xander had been at the library all night and all day, he had completely disappeared off Anya's female radar screen. Had she come down here with Justine hoping to find him? Did she have reason to think he was in trouble?

Did she deliberately leave a trail? Buffy wondered as she stood up and surveyed the broken line of long depressions. It was a farfetched idea. Anya was out of the Slayer circle. She didn't know that Justine was the unwitting pawn of a Hindu goddess who wanted to destroy the universe several billion years ahead of schedule. Or that Justine planned to steal her mind to empower the fourth painting and make it happen.

Oblivion was only one Tarot reading away.

Buffy quickly made another pointer, then hurried

on down the passageway. She tracked the broken line of long marks just in case. Time was not on her side.

Wooden Wares and the old fabric store were situated half a block inside the area the police had cordoned off for the Sunnydale Sidewalk Art Festival. Giles stopped the van in the street, nose into the wooden barriers, turned off the ignition and pocketed the keys. The world could end before he found a legal parking space.

He spotted Joyce as he slipped out and slammed the door closed. She stopped pacing when he waved, then broke into a run toward them. As he turned to open the back door, a Sunnydale squad car pulled up beside him. A second car screeched to a halt behind it.

"We never see a police officer when a demon attacks, but violate a minor traffic law and they swarm." Muttering under his breath, Giles turned to confront them, hiding his anxiety as the minutes passed. "Is there a problem, officers?"

"You can't park here, buddy!" A young, uniformed cop swaggered up to him.

"Right. You gotta move it." His paunchy partner blustered. Frowning, he flipped open a citation pad. "After I write out a ticket."

"Fine. Just stick it on the windshield. I've got an emergency." Giles slid open the side door. Getting two dazed teens and one who was out cold past the overly zealous policemen without raising their suspicions would be a challenge, but he had to chance it. "Oz—help me get Xander out."

Oz slid out of the back seat and pulled on Xander's arm.

"Hey!" The younger man grabbed Giles. "You leave this car and I'm having it towed!"

Giles wrenched free. "Far be it from me to argue with the local authorities. Do what you must. Now, if you'll excuse me—"

"Giles!" Joyce ran up looking frantic. "What's going on here?" she asked the officers.

"Illegal parking, Ms. Summers." The older man touched the brim of his hat. "Do you know this guy?"

"Yes! I called him." Joyce's eyes flashed indignantly. "Go check with your captain or whoever you check with. This is—"

"—an emergency," Giles finished for her, grateful that she had the presence of mind to buy them a few minutes. He positioned himself on one side of Xander before his limp form crumpled to the ground. "Oz. Other side. Quickly, please!"

Oz obeyed without a word.

"Right!" Joyce glared at the police and waved her cell phone at the squad cars. "So—go call!"

The two officers exchanged a look, shrugged, and retired to one of the vehicles to contact the station.

"What's wrong with him?" Joyce peered into Xander's vacant eyes.

"No time to explain. I could use your help getting them out of here, however." Giles nodded toward

Willow who was slouched in the back seat. "Give her simple instructions. She'll do exactly as you say."

Nodding, Joyce stuck her head into the Citroën. "Come on, Willow. Get out."

By the time Willow emerged from the car, the two officers were on their way back—scowling.

"Did Buffy get here all right?" Giles asked quietly.

"Yes." Joyce nodded. "She went into the old store and didn't come out."

"Well, that's something." Giles retrieved his keys and tossed them to Joyce. "You have to play with the stick to get it into reverse."

"If you can manage saving the universe, I think I can handle a couple of cops and a sticky gearshift." Joyce motioned him to get going, then turned to hold off the city's finest.

Giles shifted his grip on Xander. "Willow! Oz! Walk fast."

The half-block seemed like a long mile under the curious scrutiny of artists and art show spectators as Giles and Oz dragged Xander down the sidewalk. The circumstances hardly allowed for a clandestine operation. However, they reached the alley without incident and he heaved a sigh of relief as they filed into the deserted store.

"Stop here, Oz." Giles needed a moment to get his bearings and ordered Oz to drop Xander. A minute passed before he realized Willow was still walking like a dutiful robot girl straight for a door on the far wall. "Willow, halt!"

She stopped—a mere foot from the stairs that led down into the cellar, Giles realized when he jumped toward her. He pulled her back and glanced down into the dim light of a single, grime-covered bulb. The stairs were narrow and rotted in places. Maneuvering Xander down would require some creative verbal direction to Oz.

To avoid confusion, Giles guided Willow down into the musty basement first and commanded her to stay. Five minutes later he and Oz finished wrestling Xander down with—hopefully—only minimal bumps and bruises. Winded, he dropped Xander on the basement floor and paused to catch his breath. Willow and Oz sat on command.

Giles took a moment to pull Xander's arm out from under the dead weight of his lanky frame. The boy's head rolled back and his mouth fell open. A trickle of drool smeared the dust on his chin. No visible vestige of Xander's personality remained in his limp body.

Giles peered into Oz and Willow's blank faces. They could hear him because they responded to his commands. "But are you aware of what's happening?"

He leaned toward them, hoping for some indication that they understood. Their vacant eyes stared past him, unseeing.

Since the expedition was taking longer than Giles had calculated, Giles didn't waste any more time. He guided Willow down the ladder into the tunnels and stood her off to the side. He returned to the basement level and lost another five minutes fashioning a harness from lengths of old electrical wire. Issuing precise instructions to Oz, they managed to lower Xander to the tunnel floor where he flopped on a pile of rocks.

Giles wiped his sweaty brow and sighed. None of the numerous "end of the universe" scenarios the Watchers Council had explored smacked of slapstick. Nor, of course, would any by-the-book Watcher waste time and energy to save three teenagers when the fate of the entire universe was at stake.

"At least I don't have to file a report," Giles muttered as he struggled to hoist Xander onto his shoulders.

Curious about how the marks might have been made, Buffy experimented by dragging her left foot. The resulting imprint in the dust looked the same as the shallow marks she had been following through the tunnel. Also, since none of the impressions had been disturbed by an overlying footprint, they were fresh.

"So I'm either tracking a hopping slug demon, or Anya managed to leave a trail." Buffy glanced back down the tunnel, wishing she had investigated the mark at Justine's entry point into the underground network. If the depressions in the dust began there, she'd know for sure, but she couldn't spare the time to go back. Having no other options, she picked up the pace and followed the marks—until they suddenly vanished.

Buffy stopped short and backed up slowly. The line of markers ended at a slightly elevated spot in the floor. The smooth stone surface was dust and footprint free and formed a ledge outside a narrow break in the rock wall. No light filtered through the crack, but she didn't have another lead and time was getting critical. She had never had a Tarot reading done, but it couldn't take too long.

Feeling her way with her hands, Buffy crept through the narrow passage in the dark for several feet. Her eyes soon adjusted to a dim glow cast by shiny stuff growing on the rock. She paused when she heard a muted human voice coming from a dimly lit opening, then silently eased forward.

The cavern was huge and lit by several battery-powered camp lights. Buffy scanned the scene in an instant, taking in every detail. All the paintings but one were leaning against the far wall. The last image was on an easel by the card table in the center of the natural cathedral. Anya and Justine were seated opposite each other on folding chairs.

Anya was staring into space, zapped into mindless limbo like Xander, Willow, and Oz.

Justine was talking and dealing the Tarot cards.

No! Buffy's mind lurched. *It can't be too late!* She couldn't remember what Giles had said about the mental transfer process that would empower the last painting. Was it too late once the Tarot reading had begun or not until after it was finished? *Whatever*. The world and everything in it was destined for oblivion if Justine finished the deck.

Justine's face registered surprise when she turned and saw Buffy charging toward her, then fear.

Major clue there, Buffy thought. The artist wouldn't be afraid if she was already invincible.

Turning back to Anya, Justine quickly pulled a card off the deck with a trembling hand.

A wave of hope spurred Buffy forward with a burst of lightning speed. Her hand slammed down over Justine's as the artist placed the card on the table.

A shock jolted Buffy's brain and the world began to slow down.

CHAPTER 14

Angel pressed against hard rock, his head thrown back, sweat running in rivulets along his clenched jaw.

He had been systematically combing the underground for Justine since Buffy had left that morning. The search area had narrowed when he had entered the old, secondary network under the downtown streets. The tunnels had been cleared of all the supernatural creatures that lurked and hunted within them, all of them driven away by the evil surrounding the artist.

Justine was protected from the denizens of the dark by Kali, and the effect was enhanced by her proximity to the Hellmouth.

It had taken every shred of Angel's will to resist the overwhelming urge to flee. He would not have been able to fight the powerful force at all except that he had a soul.

"Oz! Stop!"

Giles. Angel's head snapped toward the sound of the librarian's voice. If Giles and Oz were down here, then Buffy probably was, too. He reached out with his senses to probe the labyrinth beyond the four humans in the tunnel to the more potent essence of the Slayer.

The trace was faint, masked by the revolting evil that filled the passageway Buffy traveled.

Steeling himself, Angel pushed off the wall and plunged deeper into the realm of Kali's influence.

He found Giles stumbling through the tunnel dragging Xander between himself and Oz.

"Need some help?" Angel asked.

"Angel?" Startled, Giles lost his grip and Xander's limp body collapsed on the ground in a twisted heap. "Yes, please. Buffy came down ahead of us, but I don't know where she is exactly."

"I do." Fighting the debilitating effects of Kali's protective ward, Angel lifted Xander and threw him over his shoulder.

Oz was still clutching Xander's arm and Angel's sweeping movement yanked him off his feet.

"Oz. Let go." Giles exhaled with exasperation when Oz released his grip.

Angel glanced from Willow to Oz. They were obviously victims of the same coma condition as Xander, which Buffy had described to him last night. *And fading fast,* he realized.

"Willow, Oz . . . run." Giles sprinted down the dark corridor after the pair, calling back over his shoulder. "We have to hurry, Angel."

"No argument there." Angel shifted Xander's weight on his shoulder and forced his legs to move against a tide of undiluted malevolence intent on stopping him.

Buffy stared. Justine's hand was trapped between hers and the Tarot card the artist had just drawn. The tips of Buffy's fingers barely touched it.

The high pitch of Justine's alarmed cry slid into a lower register and faded out. "Noooooooo . . ."

"Where am I?" Anya snapped. "What's going on?"

Buffy swayed with dizziness as the cavern shimmered.

"Bu-fffffy!"

Angel? Buffy's head felt like it was anchored by lead weights as she turned toward the entrance. Angel dropped Xander and moved into the cavern in slow motion with Giles gliding on his heels. Willow and Oz sank to the stone floor. Anya ran to Xander with slowed, leaping strides that belied her urgency.

Then the cavern vanished in the gray fog that flooded Buffy's mind.

"Xander!" Anya raced past Giles and Angel without giving them a glance.

Focused on the Slayer, Giles stopped just short of

running into her. His heart sank as he looked into her empty eyes. *What on earth had happened?*

Oz plowed into him from behind.

"Stop!" Startled, Giles yelled. "Back five paces and—halt."

Angel had fallen to his knees at the halfway point. The vampire clutched his head in agony, his facial features a distorted mixture of human and demon. *Unfortunate and curious,* Giles thought, *but Buffy's affliction is more important.*

Straightening his glasses, Giles studied Buffy and Justine. Both were frozen in a macabre version of Statues, the children's game, while Anya had been freed from the trance state that gripped Xander, Willow, and Oz. Justine had, apparently, just dealt the last card in a simple spread. Anya's Tarot reading had not yet been completed when Buffy clamped down on the artist's hand.

Giles leaned over to get a closer look at Buffy's hand. Her fingers were touching the card drawn from Hovan's deck. There was only one conclusion to be drawn, Giles realized. The old Gypsy's Tarot cards allowed Justine to control her potential donors. The Slayer's touch had broken the link to Anya.

"The transfer . . ." Giles's gaze snapped to the painting of the Judgment card on the easel. No hints of color brightened the contrasting black and gray tones. The transfer of Buffy's emotional matrix into the last painting should be accelerated to the point of nearly instantaneous according to his calculations, but nothing was happening. *Why not?*

"Why isn't Xander moving?" Anya demanded behind him.

"Not now!" Irritated, Giles mulled over the implications of the interrupted Tarot reading. Buffy's mind should be empowering the painting, but the process seemed to be on hold. "Justine . . ."

Giles moved around the table. Buffy had trapped the artist's hand between hers and the card. It seemed feasible to assume that both conscious minds had been drawn into the realm of the Judgment card. Then why wasn't the empowerment process underway?

"*. . . the battleground where good must prevail.*" Giles's own words regarding the interpretation of the Judgment card provided the clue. *Because two minds were inserted into the painting they've both retained free will, which might also account for the delay in the actual matrix transfer.* His mind raced through the possibilities. The eternal conflict between good and evil would be fought again between Buffy and Justine.

One will prevail and escape.

The other would empower the Judgment card, finishing the deck and initiating Kali's cosmic reign of destruction.

Unless he made sure there was no deck.

Giles glanced back. Angel was trying to crawl forward, but he seemed to be in acute pain as well as pushing against an invisible barrier. *No help there,* Giles thought with dismay.

Anya sat on the floor behind Angel cradling Xander's head in her lap.

"Anya! Come here, please. Now!"

"And leave Xander lying here helpless?" Anya shook her head. "Forget it."

"Xander is going to die if you don't help me," Giles pointed out impatiently.

Xander's head thumped the floor as Anya jumped up and joined Giles several feet in front of the paintings arrayed along the back wall. "Xander is in the Death card. His mind, that is."

"In there?" Anya squinted at the black void of Death's hooded face and shuddered. "Can we get him out?"

"Yes." Giles scanned the paintings, noting that there was very little distinction between the vibrant color and fine detail in Xander's Death card and the Tower and Devil paintings that Willow and Oz occupied.

The back of Giles's neck tingled with a sudden static charge. "We must destroy the paintings. All of them. The fate of the entire universe is at stake here."

"I don't want to know, okay?" Anya shuddered. "I just want to save Xander and get out—"

Giles grabbed Anya's arm and yanked her back.

The rock floor where they had been standing turned molten red, then split open. Blue and gold flames erupted from the ground and lashed out, driving them back from the paintings.

Kali.

Searing metal and sizzling rocks spewed out from

another crack that ripped straight for Giles and Anya. "Anya, move!"

"But Xander's mind is in there!"

"If his body burns, his mind will have nowhere to go! Move!" Shielding his head with his arm, Giles drove Anya back toward the entrance.

Ever since Giles had figured out that her friends were being mentally relocated into Tarot paintings, Buffy had tried to prep herself for a detour into Tarot land. Even so, it took a few moments to adjust. It wasn't exactly her idea of a fun, getaway weekend. Sunnydale was practically "sugar and spice and everything nice" compared to the weird, distorted world inside the painting.

Wisps of yellow mist rose from pools of bubbling goop that smelled like rotten fish. Multicolored reptiles slithered around burning rocks and dead trees. Streamers of black moss hung from twisted branches that stood out in stark contrast to the sunny, blue skies above. Beautiful beings with golden wings soared through fluffy white clouds and transformed into horned demons when they swooped too close to the scorched ground.

Heaven, Hell or a combination of both? Buffy shivered and wrapped her arms around herself. Although her body was still in the cave, her mind created an illusion of form within the painting. Justine looked the same, too.

Buffy frowned as she watched Justine. The artist

wasn't supposed to be in here with her and obviously wasn't thrilled with the unexpected change in plans. Justine turned slowly, taking in the bizarre surroundings, shaking her head in disbelief.

"*. . . where good must prevail.*"

Giles's words echoed in Buffy's mind.

Prevail over what, exactly?

The sky above split open and a long golden trumpet emerged. The horn emitted a low, keening note that drove the reptiles into tormented fits. Jaws snapped at slashing tails and they devoured themselves. The winged beings were stricken with spasms and fell from the sky, shrieking.

Like the other creatures in the strange world, the sound of the distant trumpet affected Buffy's emotional center. A terrible loneliness laced with despair welled up within her.

Buffy covered her ears, but the depressing feelings did not diminish with the fading sound of the trumpet. Somehow, the surreal prison of the Judgment card was evoking and augmenting old fears and concerns that she had settled long ago.

She could never escape being the Slayer.

She knew that, had accepted it and moved on . . . but even so, she could not shake the overwhelming sense of hopeless helplessness that immutable fact instilled in her now.

The isolation of her unique status was absolute.

For her, the only way out was death.

"Buffy . . ." Angel's whispering voice called.

Buffy opened her eyes. Tall and handsome, his dark brooding eyes filled with hurt, Angel stood before her. He held out his hand. His image shimmered, then blinked out.

Gone . . .

The pain of knowing they could never really be together drove Buffy to her knees. She loved Angel with all her heart and soul as he did her, but the purity and depth of their love were the very things that kept them apart.

Her love was Angel's doom.

So she was alone.

Not quite, she realized, as a montage of images drawn from her memory appeared in gruesome detail on the smoking landscape.

Demons from her past—the vampire Master who had killed her; Eyghon, who sought to destroy Giles; the dismembered parts of the Judge; the fraternity mentor Machida; and Acathla, who had swept Angel into Hell—mocked her. She had defeated them all, but they were mere harbingers of the more powerful and insidious evils amassing within the Hellmouth.

Buffy cringed as the witches of Sunnydale faded in to dance among their demonic kin. The ancient Shugra laughed and hurled a bolt of red, primal magick. Catherine Madison emerged in a flash of indigo light. Ethan Rayne applauded from the sidelines when the hideous blob of the egg-laying Bezoar suddenly burst through the ground.

Drusilla whispered in Buffy's ear. "It's not over, yet."

Buffy shrank back. *It will never be over.* It didn't matter where she went or what she did—anyone close to her would be in constant danger.

Too many would die.

Too many *had* died.

Jenny Calendar, Stephen Platt, Dr. Gregory, Debby Foley, Principal Flutie, Herbert the pig ... the list went on and on, endlessly. . . .

The crushing guilt was more than Buffy thought she could stand.

Justine's fear of the Queen of Wands had not been unfounded. Although she had heeded the cards' warning, Buffy Summers had become a huge obstacle on the road to her ultimate goal.

Worse, Justine thought as the extent of her predicament became clear. Buffy's interference had transported her own mind into the Judgment painting, too. She shut her eyes, hoping that if she rejected the bizarre, disgusting elements of the heaven and hell she had created she would somehow be shifted back where she belonged. She refused to look when the low, mournful wail of a horn blared from above.

This isn't how it's supposed to happen!

Keeping her eyes shut, Justine threw her arms over her head to block out the disturbing sound and images. She was supposed to be in charge! When Kali's Major Arcana deck was finished she would have everything she wanted with the mere flip of a card, everything she could never have attained on her own.

The thought reverberated through Justine's disembodied mind with staggering intensity. Truth trampled the flimsy blockade of self-denial.

She had never doubted her talent. Her teachers as far back as elementary school had encouraged her remarkable abilities, but none had understood her stubborn interest in the fantastic. As a child they excused her imaginative creatures and magical scenes as a phase she'd outgrow. Her instructors had not been so forgiving in art school. Such self-indulgence, they said, was a waste of her talent because the fine-art world would never take fantasy seriously.

She had switched to sofa-art seascapes in decorator color schemes and portraits so she could make a passable living—until she had discovered Hovan's notes and Tarot deck. With the power of the Kali Major Arcana her ancestors had been too cowardly to create, she would attain respect and financial security with her fantasy work . . . success she hadn't been willing to work for on her own, win or lose.

A vision snapped into Justine's mind, a self-portrait stripped of the façade she had adopted. Gaunt and skeletal, she saw herself for what she was: a creature without substance, hollow and bitter, seeking vengeance on the innocent for her own shortcomings. Moaning in torment, Justine collapsed.

"You must fight or die," a coarse, low voice hissed. "You are my chosen—"

"Kali?" Justine opened her eyes. A red lizard with turquoise eyes flicked a long, forked tongue at her arm. She pulled away, jumped to her feet.

"Fight!" The voice was all around her. "Only in victory can you escape."

Bolstered by the presence of the dark goddess, Justine pushed her self-doubt aside and focused on Buffy. The Queen of Wands cowered in trembling agony, locked in personal combat with her own inner demons.

Perhaps, Justine thought, *this is how it's supposed to be, after all.* Judgment was nothing less than the battle between good and evil.

In the end only one would prevail and escape the Tarot.

Justine grinned. Buffy couldn't win against the power of Kali.

Willow listened to the scraping sound of the huge stones closing in on her from all sides. She had been sitting inside the dark tower completely out of touch with the real world for what seemed like days but was probably only hours. She had kept alert with a modicum of perk by running over spells in her mind and assuring herself that Giles and Buffy were working on a way to set her, Oz, and Xander free. Now, suddenly, her relatively safe position as an observer within the Tarot world changed.

Something slimy slithered over her hand.

"Not fun!" Willow jumped to her feet and shivered as another storm engulfed the massive edifice. The flash of lightning was visible through slits that appeared high in the stone walls. *Stone walls that are moving,* she realized as her eyes adjusted to the erratic bursts of light.

Willow quickly determined that she could either stand still and be crushed or climb onto the moving stone. She climbed. The instant she was clear of the floor, the stones slid together with a crash. In the next instant, the stones at the base of the new floor began to press inward.

Faced with the same two options again, Willow climbed. "Like I have a choice," she muttered as the stones forced her upward to the pinnacle of the tower. She was being herded again, just as she had been when the lightning strikes had forced her to retreat into the tower in the first place.

Just like she had allowed herself to be bullied and manipulated in real life. Not always, but more often than she liked to admit.

Like when Principal Snyder wouldn't take no for an answer about tutoring Percy. Willow frowned. The disturbing train of thought was set aside when it looked like she would be crushed between the last floor and the ceiling. However, as the top tier of stones moved inward, the ceiling stones recessed to reveal a dark, roiling sky. Tendrils of blue and gold lightning sprang from crimson clouds above her. Thunder rumbled and cracked, shaking the tower.

At least it's not acid raining, Willow thought as she huddled on the stone platform high above the flat terrain that stretched unbroken toward the horizon. She waited for what might happen next, hoping there was no next.

Not very likely. Something had triggered the tower to alter itself, Willow reasoned. She hadn't done anything that could account for it. *But maybe Buffy did!*

The elation Willow felt at that possibility vanished when the rock beneath her shifted and cracked. She realized the stone floor beneath her could suddenly recess *back* into the walls, which would leave her hanging in midair. *For about a split second before I plunge to my death on the ground. Don't think so.*

Willow leaped for the wall that ringed the top of the tower just as the floor dropped out from under her. Sharp stone edges cut into her hands as she clung to the cold, damp stone watching skeletons and partially decomposed bodies emerge from the wall. One by one they dove off the tower, screaming until they impacted on the hard ground.

Willow hung on, her fingers bleeding and cramped with cold, fighting an overwhelming urge to throw herself screaming off the tower.

Instinctively, she knew that the moment she hit

the ground in the Tarot world, she would die in her real life.

The taunting, accusing images were relentless in their attack. Buffy tried to run from them, but the distorted world of the Tarot shifted the landscape so she was running in circles. Haunted and hunted by the violence of her past, she fell on her knees and began digging in the sand. Since she couldn't run from the memories that pursued her, she would bury them so they couldn't rise to plague her again.

The dead don't remember.

Granules of glass stung Buffy's palms and salty tears stung her eyes. The angry apparitions drawn from her past formed a ring around her, taunting her as she worked. Sand seeped in to fill up the hole as fast as she scooped it out. Furious and frustrated, she clenched her fists and started to scream.

The sound never left her throat.

A sudden burst of insight stopped Buffy's self-destructive plunge into insanity.

The Tarot was pitting her against herself.

Buffy drew a long, calming breath and brushed a strand of tangled hair off her face. The nature of Tarot was to create a state of self-examination that would enlighten. *Or in the case of Kali's deck,* she realized, *to condemn.*

She couldn't hide from herself, her past, or her future without rejecting her Slayer identity.

And being the Slayer was a sacred trust she would never abandon, even if she could.

Screeching in defeat, the images blinked out one by one.

Renewed strength flowed from an inner reservoir to re-energize Buffy's sense of self. She did not have to apologize for or defend her actions.

But I do have to defend myself, she thought as Justine's narrowed gaze snapped to meet hers. Apparently, the artist had just finished a couch session with her own psychic demons and was ready to fight for her survival.

Buffy braced herself as Justine advanced. Although surprised, she didn't flinch when a gross, vaguely female countenance superimposed itself over the artist's form.

"Kali, I presume?" Buffy asked, but she had no doubt. The dark goddess looked exactly as Giles had described her, and it wasn't hard to understand why Kali had it in for the universe. She was clearly a contender for "most hideous" among the ugly, disgusting demons Buffy had previously encountered.

Kali was an emaciated hag with long, black tangled hair that fanned behind her in wild disarray. Piercing black eyes burned in an angular face accented by dripping, crimson fangs. She wore a necklace of skulls and carried a blood-soaked sword in one of her eight hands. Hundreds of metal bracelets jangled on her arms and shrunken heads dangled from her belt.

On a fashion scale of one to ten, Buffy gave her a retrospective eight. The "Bloodthirsty Barbarian" look hadn't been in since the fifth century and Attila the Hun. Marveling at the bit of high school history trivia she had retained, Buffy subtly shifted her weight to repel an attack.

The image of Kali vanished as Justine snarled and lunged. Presumably untrained in combat, the artist moved with a speed and agility that caught Buffy off guard. She staggered as Justine plowed into her, recovered, and kicked. Her foot barely missed her mark as Justine jumped clear, whirled, and landed a brutal blow at the base of Buffy's neck, which dropped her to her knees.

Reeling, Buffy shook her head, then ducked and rolled to avoid another powerful strike. Leaping to her feet, she circled her sneering opponent. Justine held her gaze, confident that she could easily smash her foe. Kali's image had disappeared, but the powerful goddess had clearly not abandoned her pawn. She and Justine were evenly matched in a brawl to the death.

Matching Justine's superior stare, Buffy smiled, disarming the empowered artist for a moment. She had already won the ultimate battle when she had prevailed against the darker side of her own nature. Infused with Kali's power, Justine might win the battle of good and evil, but she could never get Buffy to surrender.

She was the Slayer.

CHAPTER 15

Behind Giles, flames and hot bits of brimstone continued to shoot out of the rift. Kali had probably created a fire wall to keep them away from the paintings, as the paintings now appeared impervious to heat and flame. Although the dark goddess could not physically breach the Hellmouth barrier, he believed her powerful rage had broken through. He could barely make out the still forms of Buffy and Justine beyond the roaring fire, but they, too, were unaffected by the inferno.

"Shouldn't we retreat?" Anya asked.

"Yes, good idea." Giles turned to see Willow and Oz standing where he had left them. "Willow! Oz! Run back!"

Angel was on his hands and knees, staring into the fire that surrounded Buffy.

"Get back, Angel!" Giles yelled as he ran. Ahead of him, Oz suddenly collapsed. Anya zoomed by him and Willow. Willow was walking, he noted with chagrin, but at least she was moving under her own power.

Giles dropped to one knee by Oz and quickly felt for a pulse. He was alive, but had finally fallen into a coma. A blast of ball lightning zoomed over his head. It barely missed Willow and slammed into the wall in an explosive burst of blue-white light.

"Look out!" Anya pointed, then threw herself on top of Xander, who was stretched out on the floor.

"Willow! Duck!" Giles flattened himself over Oz while keeping one eye on the dazed girl.

Willow's response time lagged by seconds. Stumbling back toward the entrance, Angel grabbed Willow's leg and toppled her. The sphere of energy barely missed her head as she fell, but tendrils of electricity radiating off the supercharged projectile singed her hair.

"Down! Stay down!" Giles belly-crawled forward dragging Oz by the wrist.

Willow folded into a still lump on the floor.

Out cold or merely following instructions—literally? Giles inched up beside Angel and the fallen girl. He shook her shoulder, but she did not react. The absorption process was accelerating just as he had suspected. "Angel—"

The vampire's tormented gaze was riveted on the inferno. On the far side of the raging fire, Buffy was on her feet, and Justine was still frozen in her chair. The showdown within the painting wasn't over, yet.

"Angel!" Giles shouted and shook him, but the vampire had also, apparently, fallen into a state of catatonia.

"Anya!" Giles rose on one elbow. "I could use your help here."

"I'm not leaving Xander!" Anya flattened, shielding Xander from another lightning strike.

"Of course," Giles muttered. "Heaven forbid something should happen to the rest of us." Rolling Oz onto his side, Giles pulled Willow to the wall first. A lightning ball detonated above him, showering him with sparks. The stone at the point of impact turned black and smoldered.

"There's an overhang over there." Giles pointed to a ledge beyond the entrance. "It might afford us some protection."

"Fine." Anya craned her neck to look. "Xander first."

"I think it might be prudent to retrieve Oz first, don't you?" Giles asked. Her devotion to Xander was charming, but incredibly inconvenient most of the time. At the moment, Xander was as safe as possible under the circumstances. Oz was in imminent danger.

"All right." Anya crouched to run.

A loud boom reverberated through the cavern.

Giles looked back as a stream of molten rock and metal oozed through a break in the rock floor a few feet from Oz's position. Just as Giles was about to charge forward, Angel struggled to his feet and clamped onto Oz's wrist.

"Over there, Angel!" Giles waved toward the ledge on the far side of the entrance. Dragging Oz, Angel hobbled for the wall with the ground splitting open at his heels. Giles turned to pick up Willow.

"Help," Anya grunted. She couldn't budge Xander and blindsided Giles with big, brown eyes. "Please?"

"Yes, well—quickly, then." Slipping his arms under Xander's shoulders, Giles hauled him to the ledge. Leaving Anya with Angel to help get Xander under cover, Giles darted back to Willow. He scooped her slim body into his arms and turned away as a large chunk of rock crashed where she had lain.

With everyone safe and jammed into the tight indentation under the rocky overhang, Giles turned his attention back to the chaos Kali had unleashed. Screaming tornadoes ripped through the cavern slicing rock and drawing fire into swirling funnels. Ball lightning rampaged and the molten streams widened and pooled.

"Shouldn't we just get out of here?" Anya shouted in Giles's ear.

"No! Xander must be near the painting when it's destroyed or he'll die!" Giles motioned toward the paintings lined up along the wall on the far side of the cavern. A storm of fire and falling rock raged around them, but they remained unharmed.

"Great! We can't even get near them!" Anya scowled.

"Maybe I can." Angel inched forward.

"I don't think so," Giles said. "Something in this cavern is having an adverse affect on you. Buffy would never forgive me if I let you burn."

"If she lives." Angel's gaze snapped back to the Slayer.

"She will." Giles glanced toward the blazing center of the inferno. Buffy, Justine, and the Judgment painting remained in a bubble of calm at the center of the storm.

"She's not exactly tackling this problem with her usual reckless gusto." Anya scoffed and glared at the immobile Slayer.

"I beg to differ." Giles allowed himself a slight smile. "Buffy is putting up rather a good fight. In fact, I daresay she's winning."

"Winning?" Anya arched an eyebrow, her tone sarcastic. "And you're basing that assumption on what?"

Giles motioned toward the rampaging elements. "Kali is throwing a tempest tantrum."

"A lot of good that does Xander," Anya huffed.

"Don't you ever give up?" Xander stared at the hooded manifestation of Death that had relentlessly stalked him across the barren desert for the past several hours. "Or talk?"

The Grim Reaper moved forward without a word, the cadence of its steady pace unbroken.

Xander eased out from behind the boulder where he had tried to hide. To no avail again. Death had dogged and found him without fail. No matter where or how far he had gone, it just kept coming.

"Kind of like the real thing," Xander muttered as he moved out along the base of the ridge. Jagged peaks unadorned by brush or tree or even a blade of grass rose into a gray, cloudless sky.

Spotting what looked like the darkened entrance to a cave, Xander broke into a jog. *Why bother?* he wondered. The black entity under the hood would just keep coming. *Until it catches me. And then what?*

Maintaining a pace that put a little distance between himself and Reaper Man, Xander tried to puzzle it out. In Tarot, death didn't necessarily mean Death. *Change based on destruction, yes, but not the big end-all. Then again, this isn't your ordinary Tarot.*

Stumped, Xander slowed to a walk and glanced over his shoulder. The distance between him and the dark figure was the same. *No,* he realized. The distance had closed—a lot. *Which means what? That I'm running out of time?*

Faced with the possibility that death really did mean *Death* within Justine's Tarot painting, Xander broke into a faster jog, his thoughts racing. He assumed Giles, Buffy, Willow and Oz were working on getting him out. If they succeeded, then no problem. If they didn't, he was doomed to keep running for his life until the end of time.

Which sort of describes my real life, too. No mat-

ter where I go or what I do, I can't get away from my real self. Present circumstances excepted, he thought, referring to his confinement in the Tarot painting. *Not an acceptable alternative.*

Xander stopped in front of the cave and peered inside. He couldn't tell what lay in the total darkness beyond the entrance. Like the future that stretched before him, the interior of the cave was unseen and unknown. And it filled him with dread.

Which might explain why I don't want to grow up and leave childish things behind. Like water balloon fights and detention for chewing gum in class or worrying about having a date for the prom. I should give all that up? For what? A mortgage and quarterly job performance reports? Xander stared into the cave for another moment, then turned away.

To find the Grim Reaper had gotten a lot closer a lot faster.

Xander swallowed hard, then froze when he realized the ridge had shifted position to effectively cut off his escape. He was left with two choices: brave the scary unknown dark in the cave or confront Death.

Oddly enough, death was inescapable regardless of which option he chose. It was just a matter of sooner or later.

As Xander gazed into the infinite black shrouded by the Grim Reaper's hood, he was suddenly certain of one thing. Something he had avoided thinking about since his whole bizarre adventure in Tarotland had started.

If the figure caught him, he *would* die.

Justine fought with the ferocity of a crazed animal. She kicked and flailed to pull free of Buffy's stranglehold.

Exhausted, bruised, and bleeding, Buffy held on through the force of her own will. Justine's strength and determination, enhanced by Kali, had made her more than an equal match. Although Buffy's body didn't physically exist within the painting, she had felt the effects of every blow, scratch, and gouge Justine delivered. The sustained struggle was starting to wear her down and the artist knew it.

Buffy flinched when Justine raked her cheek with hard, perfectly manicured nails and her grip loosened. She let go when Justine's teeth sank into her arm.

Justine whirled and rammed her.

Buffy lurched back, tripped, and fell. The impact forced the imagined air from her lungs, stunning her.

Crouched to attack, Justine smiled through her snarl. "Give it up, Buffy."

Breathless, Buffy couldn't answer. She focused on Justine's narrowed gaze. If the artist pounced now, Buffy realized, she wouldn't be able to defend herself. She couldn't even move to shake off the huge blue snake slithering up her leg. However, Justine's arrogant pause bought her precious seconds.

"You'll exist in this hell forever, Buffy." Justine kicked a lizard into a putrid pool of steaming green gunk. The creature screamed as it scrambled out. Its shimmering red scales were charred black and began to flake. Justine laughed. "You can't win, Buffy."

"Actually—" Buffy's hand whipped out and closed around the snake. Glittering yellow eyes blinked with surprise as she hurled it into the air, then leaped to her feet. "—I can't lose."

Justine took an uncertain step back. "Wrong. You're no match for Kali."

"Probably not." Buffy shrugged, unconcerned. "But there's a big difference between taking on the *real* Kali and fighting a surrogate."

"Kali is here." Justine thumped her chest with her fist. "With me."

"Which has given you a remarkable advantage, I admit," Buffy said, "but it's still *you* in *your* virtual body, Justine, and Kali can't prop you up forever." She was painfully aware that the advantage was real, but it couldn't hurt to try and drive a wedge into Justine's confidence. Neither one of them had a physical presence within the Tarot painting. They were both relying on the inner strength of their personalities.

"Don't count on it," Justine sneered.

"I won't." Buffy struck quickly and surely, planting a swift kick to the artist's chest. The blow staggered the woman, but she stayed on her feet. Buffy followed through with a left hook to the jaw.

Enraged, Justine lowered her head and charged, slamming Buffy into a large boulder.

Pain shot up Buffy's spine. She raised her arm to block a blow and Justine kicked her in the stomach. Buffy locked her legs around the artist and flipped backward, throwing the woman over her head to the ground.

Scrambling to her feet, Justine fell back out of range and began to circle.

Clamping her hand to a large bruise in her side, Buffy matched the maneuver, buying some recovery time. In truth, she didn't stand a chance with Kali in the equation. As long as Justine believed she was invincible, she was.

So I'll just have to convince her she isn't, Buffy thought as Justine suddenly barreled toward her. Buffy jumped aside, but the artist anticipated the move, dodged, and drove her to the ground.

Buffy's head struck a rock, stunning her for a few critical seconds.

Driven by the wrath of raw evil, Justine grabbed Buffy by the hair and flung the dazed Slayer against the jagged surface of a tall stone.

Battered and bleeding, Buffy drew herself into a ball to protect herself from Justine's kicks. *But it's obviously not going to be easy,* she thought as nausea and dizziness added to her misery.

CHAPTER 16

Oz had given up fighting. All he had accomplished was to cut deep gouges into his wrists and ankles with the manacles. More than that, his struggles had amused the winged demon guarding him. The creature hadn't laughed once since he had been sitting quietly with his eyes closed, contemplating his predicament, the universe, and everything.

Now, apparently, the demon had grown bored and would no longer tolerate his strategy of passive resistance.

It worked for Gandhi, Oz reminded himself when he felt something twine around his arm. A burning, stinging sensation ripped through his skin where the tendril touched. The pain was similar to that of the stinging nettle he had touched on a vacation in

Florida years and years ago. He had no soap and water to relieve the discomfort now. He kept his eyes closed, gritted his teeth, and imagined a cooling waterfall.

More stinging vines twined around his legs and grew until his whole body felt like it was on fire.

Oz hummed the melody of the Dingoes' latest tune. The slow dirge quality of the song served as a suitable mantra to help him focus within and ignore that which was without. He could and would withstand anything he had to while he waited to be freed. There was no physical pain the Tarot could inflict that could possibly be worse than the emotional trauma of betraying Willow.

The thought of Willow jarred him from his meditative state. He couldn't stand the thought of her being alone and tormented within the Tower of Justine's Tarot.

And because he couldn't stand it, that's all he could think about.

In agony from the burning vines that covered his skin and the guilt that engulfed his soul, Oz cried aloud.

He would rather die than hurt Willow.

"Good, because soon you *will* die." The demon laughed.

Buffy was not as hurt as she had led Justine to believe. The element of surprise, she hoped, would throw the artist off long enough to pound another wedge into her vulnerable psyche.

Groaning, Buffy tried to crawl away from the force of Justine's battering boots.

"Had enough yet, Buffy?" Justine asked, her tone mocking.

"No, not just yet." Buffy rolled onto her side, grabbed Justine's ankle, and yanked the artist off her feet. She sprang into a fighting stance before the woman hit the ground.

Justine scrambled upright, her gaze hard and her lip curled in a snarl. "You'll pay for that."

"I'm ready whenever you are." Buffy raised her fists and smiled. The final stage of the empowerment process would not begin until one of them had vacated the virtual premises. She had found Justine's weakness and struck the first of her fatal, verbal blows. "You couldn't make it in the real world, could you, Justine?"

"What?" Justine hesitated. "I was doing just fine."

"Right, traveling from one sidewalk art show to another, never even getting invited to do a small town gallery show." Buffy shook her head. "You're a loser, Justine."

"That's a lie!" Infuriated, Justine lunged.

Buffy ducked the attack and whirled, landing a solid kick in the middle of Justine's back. The force sent Justine sprawling on the ground. "I know who *I* am, Justine. Who are you?"

Justine jumped to her feet. "I am going to be the most respected artist in the world!"

"Which will be worth nothing," Buffy retorted.

"I've devoted my whole life to my art!" Justine countered.

"And when things didn't work out the way you wanted, you sold your soul to Kali." Buffy advanced slowly, her eyes narrowed. "Everything you could have been is gone. Kali owns you. She never intended to keep her part of the bargain."

"No, that's not true! She promised—"

"She's *evil*. They don't keep their promises." Buffy pressed. "You lost this fight a long time ago—"

"No, it can't be true—" Suddenly panicked, Justine glanced about her with wild eyes. She shook her head in a frantic display of denial.

Bingo, Buffy thought. In a single moment of absolute doubt, Justine had broken her tenuous connection with Kali's essence.

Buffy swayed as the sharp outlines of rock and reptile became fuzzy. Justine fell to her knees before the transparent visage of Kali that rose out of the parched ground. A shriek of vile rage shattered the eerie landscape and receded as Buffy was swept from the scene.

Buffy's swift return to her body left her momentarily disoriented. Surrounded by flames and pelted by falling rocks, she fought to get her bearings. Justine was slumped over at the table, but Buffy's first thought was for Giles and her friends. She anxiously scanned the cave. Fire and smoke obstructed her view, but she finally found them huddled in a stone recess near the entrance. Even Angel.

Giles raised his hands to his mouth. He shouted, but she couldn't hear him over the roar of the fire and rampaging tornado winds. She turned, looking for a break in the flames. Her gaze snapped to the Judgment painting on the easel.

Vibrant color flowed across the black and gray images on the canvas.

Justine's essence was empowering the last card in Kali's doomsday deck.

"I choose you, Slayer," Kali's grating voice whispered.

Buffy's heart lurched. With the ultimate Tarot at her command, the dark goddess could, apparently, usurp another human host and still destroy the universe. *Not on my watch!*

"Sorry. I have other plans." Buffy dashed through the fire, ignoring the heat that blistered her skin. She grabbed the painting and shoved it into the flames. It didn't burn. She pulled it back and smashed it against the ground. It didn't break.

The elements were under Kali's control and could not be used against her.

But she doesn't control me.

Desperate and determined, Buffy leaned the painting against the table. An invisible brush seemed to be filling in the details, adding tones and shadings that were bringing the Judgment scene to life. She had seconds to destroy it, no more.

Buffy reacted on instinct and pulled a stake from her back pocket. Mr. Pointy was imprinted with the

Slayer's psychic signature. Kali had no power over it.

Clutching the stake in both hands, she slashed downward. The wooden point tore through the canvas. She slashed again and again, shredding the painting.

Kali's maddened screams resounded off the cavern walls as the Hellmouth reclaimed that which belonged to it. Wind, fire, and lightning were sucked into the rift like air rushing into a vacuum.

"Buffy!" Giles yelled.

Barely able to hear him, Buffy looked back. Giles waved and pointed toward the far wall. She understood immediately.

"They must be destroyed before the rift closes!"

Buffy didn't take time to acknowledge Giles. With stake still in hand, she leaped through the rift. The force of the Hellmouth's inhalation snagged her just as she touched the far side. The stake dropped from her hand as she clawed the stone floor to keep from being dragged into the underworld chasm. Inching her way back onto solid ground, she retrieved Mr. Pointy and lunged for the three paintings that imprisoned her friends. Although it was too late to save Justine's previous eighteen victims, Willow, Xander, and Oz could still be reunited with their stolen minds. She ripped and tore at the first canvas in a frenzy of destruction until a shimmering gold mist zipped out and shot across the cavern. She quickly moved on to the second and didn't stop until nothing remained of the Devil, Death, and the Tower but tatters.

As the maelstrom of fire and wind began to die down, Buffy's gaze followed Willow's speeding essence. Giles, Anya, and Angel had pulled Xander, Willow, and Oz out from under the ledge. A golden aura settled over Willow and faded as it was absorbed. All three of her friends came to with a start and struggled to stand on shaky legs. Relieved, Buffy methodically attacked the remaining paintings.

At the table, Justine looked up, still dazed by her sudden release from the ruined Judgment painting. Terror instantly replaced confusion when a wind snapped up Hovan's Tarot deck and whisked the cards into the air.

Still slashing canvas, Buffy winced as the small Tarot cards whipped around Justine, slicing her face and arms with edges made razor sharp by speed.

Justine burst out of the chair to run, but there was no escape from the covenant she had signed with Kali. The Hellmouth held her fast, drawing her and the Hovan deck into its dark maw. Her screams were silenced as the breach slammed closed.

Buffy finished shredding the last painting and dropped it. Weary to the marrow, she sagged against the wall, then started when luminescent, golden wisps began to rise from the pile of torn canvas. She watched the freed souls ascend in quiet reflection, at peace with the world and herself.

"Well, that was exciting." Anya's voice carried in the cavernous quiet.

"Nerve-racking doesn't even begin to describe it," Xander said weakly. "Death is not a fun guy."

Anya beamed. "Well, just so you know, I kept your body safe and sound."

Xander blinked. "You did?"

"So, can we go out sometime? I think you owe me." Anya asked hopefully.

"Out? Like on a real date?" Xander held up a hand. "Rewind that. The unknown isn't necessarily a bad thing, right? Let's just say I'll seriously consider it."

"When?" Anya asked.

Oz placed his hands on Willow's arms. "You know that Justine made—"

Willow placed her finger on his mouth. "Not a problem."

Oz frowned. "I would never want anything bad to happen to you."

"I can't die. Not anytime soon anyway." Willow grinned. "There's too much I want to do. Magick and college and kicking demon butt with Buffy and probably a lot of other stuff I haven't thought of yet."

"So—" Xander clapped his hands together. "Anyone up for stuffing face with tacos?"

"I am!" Anya grinned.

Buffy smiled and pocketed her stake.

Her friends had survived their ordeal with their quirky personalities intact, and the universe was back on schedule for total annihilation several billion years in the future.

And the future is tamper-proof again—for the time being, at least—which is good, Buffy thought as she caught Angel's eye. He gestured toward the break back into the tunnel. She nodded and slipped away to follow him.

I'd rather be surprised.

ABOUT THE AUTHOR

Diana G. Gallagher lives in Florida with her husband, Marty Burke, three dogs, three cats, and a cranky parrot. A Hugo Award-winning artist, she is best known for her series *Woof: The House Dragon*. Dedicated to the development of the solar system's resources, she has contributed to this effort by writing and recording songs that promote and encourage humanity's movement into space.

Her first adult novel, *The Alien Dark*, appeared in 1990. She and Marty co-authored *The Chance Factor*, a STARFLEET ACADEMY VOYAGER book. In addition to other STAR TREK novels for intermediate readers, Diana has written many books in other series published by Minstrel Books and Archway Paperbacks, including *The Secret World of Alex Mack, Are You Afraid of the Dark, The Journey of Allen Strange*, and *Sabrina the Teenage Witch*. She has two previous *Buffy the Vampire Slayer* novels published and is currently working on additional ideas for Pocket Pulse.

TV YOU CAN READ

Your favorite shows on WB are now your favorite books.

Look for books from Pocket Pulse™ based on these hit series:

ANGEL™

Buffy the vampire slayer™

Charmed™

Dawson's Creek™

ROSWELL™

Everyone's got his demons....

ANGEL™

If it takes an eternity, he will make amends.

❖

**Original stories based
on the TV show
Created by Joss Whedon
& David Greenwalt**

**Available from Pocket Pulse
Published by Pocket Books**